The Weekend Wife

Toni Blake

The Weekend Wife was originally published in a slightly different form under the title *Hotbed Honey* in 2000.

Copyright © 2000, 2017 Toni Blake.

All rights reserved.

No part of this book may be reproduced in any form or by any electronic or mechanical means, including information storage and retrieval systems, without written permission from the author, except for the use of brief quotations in a book review.

www.toniblake.com

This is a work of fiction. Names, characters, places, and incidents are a product of the author's imagination. Locales and public names are sometimes used for atmospheric purposes. Any resemblance to actual people, living or dead, or to businesses, companies, events, institutions, or locales is completely coincidental.

The Weekend Wife/ Toni Blake – 2nd ed.

To Joni Lang,
my friend, fellow writer and frequent partner in crime, who once shoved a couple of Harlequin Temptation novels into my hand and said, "You should try writing romance."

Chapter One

"I NEED A woman."

"Don't we all."

"I don't need a woman for *that*." Max Tate cast a dry look at Frank Marsallis. Then he took a sip of the scotch Frank had just shoved into his hand. "If I want *that*, I can get it. I need a partner for a job."

Frank lifted one stubby finger in the air as he gave a somber nod. "Ah—I should've known you weren't here just to crash my party."

Standing in Frank's lavish entryway, Max took an absent look across the expansive space his one-time mentor called a living room. Stylish-looking people stood in clusters drinking trendy cocktails as a slow, bluesy tune cascaded from speakers hidden in the vaulted ceiling. Not really his scene, or at least not by choice. All things considered, he'd rather be having a beer at a neighborhood bar. Especially considering the way he looked at the moment. "Crashing parties isn't my style, Frank. Anyway, the job starts tomorrow."

Frank stroked his salt-and-pepper beard, his gaze

landing on his fellow P.I. "Nothing like waiting 'til the last minute, Max."

But he didn't have time to deal with Frank's annoyance. "Look, I've been busy with a job that went longer than planned. Can you help me or not?"

"One question first. Why do you look like you've been living in a trash can?"

"Like I said, I've been busy. I just came from doing a little undercover work." Undercover assignments were his specialty.

"As what?"

"A garbage man." He slanted Frank a look of warning. "And no cracks please—I don't have time for your wit right now. I need to know if you can get me the woman."

"All right, all right," Frank said, offering an exaggerated sigh. "What are the parameters?"

"She needs to be quick-thinking," Max told him, glad to get down to business. "And she has to have good instincts. She should also be a decent actress."

"Anything else?"

Max snapped his fingers. He'd almost forgotten the most important part. "Yeah. She has to be drop-dead gorgeous."

Frank shook his graying head—either in irritation or judgment, Max couldn't tell—then returned to the matter at hand. "So why do you need a good actress?"

"She's going to pretend to be my wife."

"And why does she have to be gorgeous?"

"Same reason."

Frank cast him yet another cutting look, but this time Max turned a sly grin toward his friend. "Actually, the job calls for it, Frank, in a big way. The guy I'm trying to nail only goes after extremely hot women."

Frank took the last sip of his drink and lowered his glass to a nearby table. "So she'll be bait."

Max knew Frank didn't like the sound of that, but it was often the nature of the business for women who chose this line of work. "Something like that. That's where the quick-thinking and good instincts come in. Besides, I'll be there the whole time—either out in the open or in hiding, keeping an eye on things."

Max waited impatiently as Frank sighed again, scanning the room. If Frank couldn't come through for him on this, he was sunk. In between stints of playing garbage man, he'd spent the last two weeks drawing Carlo Coletti into this scheme, and he'd made it clear to Carlo that not only was he loaded, but that he had a beautiful wife to shower his riches on. Without one, the whole case would flop. And Frank was the only guy in town he trusted enough to borrow another P.I. from. He knew from experience that Frank hired only the best.

Frank's head suddenly darted around to face him. "I thought you were quitting." It sounded suspiciously like an accusation.

Max tilted his head derisively. "Not quitting, Frank. Stepping back. Growing the business. Bringing in some new blood."

"Quitting," Frank repeated.

Well, so what if he was? He'd been up to his ears in this business for fifteen years—since he was twenty years old, for God's sake. He'd had his own firm for the last three of those years, and now he finally had the money to hire enough good people that he could get out of the field himself. He liked the work and was damn good at it, but he'd fallen into it accidentally all those years ago and had now decided to see what it was like to have a job where he didn't risk his life every single day. So he planned to *manage* the P.I.s he'd soon hire, be the brains behind the operation and let someone else be the brawn—*and the garbage men*—for a change.

"Anyway," Max said, "I just finished up the garbage gig, so this next one is my last case. Worth a tidy fee if I can pull it off. But like I said, I need a woman. Do you have one for me?"

Frank gestured across the room. "See the brunette in the blue dress?"

Did he ever. She stood with her back to them, talking with another woman as they studied an impressionist print that hung above Frank's fireplace. She had legs that went on forever, silky hair that fell in waves past her shoulders, and a nice shape inside that dress to back it all up.

Even without seeing her face, Max knew she was a beauty—just what he was looking for. So he didn't hesitate—he looked at Frank and winked. "I'll take her."

"OKAY, KIMBERLY—THIS is the place. Number 11. Go on in and introduce yourself. I'll park the car and join you in a minute."

Kimberly Brandt stepped out of Frank's vintage mint-condition 1977 gold Cadillac into the lightly falling rain. She slammed the door, blotting out the sounds of B.B. King inside and hurried up the front steps of the stylish condo where Frank's friend lived.

Ringing the doorbell, she realized she didn't even know the guy's name. All she knew was that Frank had volunteered her to be the fellow P.I.'s wife for a few days—which sounded possibly complicated, but interesting, too. She'd done plenty of undercover work, but since joining Frank's agency, she usually worked alone. This might be a challenging change. Perhaps even fun. And good training for cases that required a team approach.

She rang the doorbell again and pulled the thin, beaded shawl she wore tighter around her shoulders as the rain began to seep in. *Come on, buddy—answer the door.*

Frank had also told her she was going to be used as bait for a thief who liked to seduce his victims before robbing them. That part *wouldn't* be so fun. But she could handle it. She'd gotten skilled at her job over the past few years.

"Damn it," she murmured, pressing the doorbell down once more, holding it for a few seconds this time. She could be a perfectly tough chick when necessary, but she didn't enjoy standing out in the rain for no good reason. If she didn't get inside soon, her linen dress would just be one big wad of wrinkles.

She glanced up and down the rain-slick sidewalk, irritated. Where was Frank? Was this guy even home? According to Frank, he'd headed home to clean up after an undercover operation, but where was he? If it was such an emergency to meet tonight, why wasn't he opening his door and welcoming her with open arms?

On impulse, she reached down and twisted the knob.

And it opened.

More surprised than she'd expected, she let go and watched the door ease to a stop at about the halfway point. She'd only tried the knob for the hell of it—she hadn't thought it would actually get her inside. What a bozo, not even keeping his door locked.

Well. What now?

"Hello?" she called, leaning through the doorway. No answer. But there were lights on. And music playing low but potent. Old-school Pearl Jam.

She tried again. "*Hello?* I'm here with Frank Marsallis, and I'm getting soaked out here," she said, projecting her voice as she tentatively placed one foot over the threshold. "And so I'm coming inside now."

And then she was in, standing in the entryway of a dimly lit living room, suddenly assaulted with a troubling thought. *God, please let this be the right condo.*

"Julie, is that you?" a deep male voice asked from somewhere unseen.

Julie? Hardly. Maybe this *was* the wrong condo. "Um, no—not Julie," she answered. "I'm here with Frank Marsallis."

But she'd barely uttered the last sentence when a man turned the corner a few feet away—wearing nothing but a green towel around his waist. The first thing she noticed was that he had a great body, lean but slightly muscular, which was her favorite kind. The second thing she noticed was that he was…Max!

Max, who she hadn't seen since the Carpenter case. *Max*, who was just as excruciatingly handsome as ever.

Their eyes met and held. And Kimberly's heart pounded with all the conflicting memories of him that raced through her brain. It took a lot of effort, but she finally forced her mouth to close. Then she swallowed, hard.

"Oh no," Max said, shaking his head. "Oh-h-ho no. This can't be. It can't. Please tell me you're not the woman Frank sent me." He was laughing now, but not in a happy way—more like a delirious, he-couldn't-believe-his-rotten-luck kind of way.

Which made her feel lousy. But didn't surprise her. She might have loved the guy once, but that didn't mean she was any happier to see him than he was to see her. "As a matter of fact, I am."

"This is my worst nightmare," he muttered.

Oh, so it was going to be like this, huh? She glared at him. "You're not exactly my first choice of a partner, either. Or my second. Or my tenth."

He raised his eyebrows. "*You're* complaining about working with *me*? I don't believe this!"

"Well, believe it. When did you get back into town, anyway?"

"About six months ago."

She narrowed her gaze and tilted her head. "And here I thought I'd never have to see you again. What on earth brought you back?"

He returned her condescending tone. "There aren't enough good P.I. firms in this town. And I figured enough time had passed since you ruined my reputation that I could come back and open up shop here."

She sucked in her breath at the accusation. How dare he! "Ruined? *Ruined*? One little incident and you blame me for—"

"All right, what the hell's going on in here?" The booming voice forced them both to shift their gazes to Frank, who stood in the doorway, wide-eyed and soaking wet. "I could hear you two all the way out on the street. And Max—what are you doing parading around in a towel?"

"Frank, you've gotta get me another woman."

"What's wrong with this one?" Frank motioned to Kimberly with outstretched hands.

"*This one* has a habit of tipping off my suspects."

"What?" Frank blurted. "She's a good P.I., Max. And the only suitable one I've got at the moment. She'll have to do."

"*She*," Kimberly injected, planting her fists on her

hips, "is not a cut of meat on a slab, gentlemen. She's standing right here, so maybe you could quit addressing her in the third person."

Max looked at her. "You just did the same thing yourself."

She rolled her eyes. "For effect. See how annoying it sounds?"

"I still don't know why you're not wearing any clothes," Frank pointed out.

"I was in the shower," Max said. "And she came in without knocking. Which might be one thing if I were an elusive suspect, but—"

"I rang the bell three times!"

Yet he ignored her and looked back to Frank, eyes pleading. "Come on, Frank. Get me somebody else. *Anybody* else."

"I told you, there *is* nobody else. I only have two other women who fit the bill, and they're already in the middle of other cases." Frank took a step toward Max. "Look, Kimberly will do a good job for you—she's never let me down."

Max eyed her critically and she knew he was remembering it again—the Carpenter case. And she wanted to cringe, but instead she just kept scowling at him. She was a much better P.I. than he'd ever given her credit for and she wouldn't let herself be cowed into guilt or submission by his accusing look.

"Never let you down, huh?" Max said, sounding as if he didn't believe a word of it.

"No," Frank said pointedly. "Now how do you two know each other, anyway?"

Max held his gaze on her. "We used to work together."

She didn't look away. "But then we got fired."

"*Both* of us," Max reiterated. "Because *she* tipped off an embezzler that we were onto her."

"An incident which I've never had the opportunity to give my version of."

But he was shaking his head and she could see that he still wasn't interested in her side of the story, even three years later, so she'd be damned if she was going to waste her time trying to make him listen. "Look, do you want me for the job or not, Tate?"

He sighed, muttering beneath his breath, "Talk about being between a rock and a hard place."

"Believe me, this is hardly my dream scenario either. But I'm a professional and I can handle it. If *you* can't, say so, and I'll happily be on my way."

She waited for his answer, her heart in her throat. She didn't know why. Or maybe she did. It was more than a little surprising to her, but maybe she really *wanted* this now, suddenly—the chance to work with him again, the chance to clear her name with him. Maybe she wanted to show the pompous, arrogant jerk just how good she was, once and for all. She'd never thought she'd have the opportunity to do that, and suddenly, here it was, laid out before her on a proverbial silver platter.

Still, he said nothing, and she wasn't about to beg, or even let him know she had anything to gain by this at all.

So after waiting for what she decided was a reasonable length of time, she turned to leave. Working with him would only be torture anyway. "Come on, Frank. Let's go back to your party. Maybe there are still some hors d'oeuvres left."

"Wait." The voice came from Max. And made her chest tighten in some combination of victory and nervousness. The old adage came back to her: *Be careful what you wish for.*

Nonetheless, she smiled inside at the idea of making him crumble by threatening to leave. It was good to see him squirm a little—and though most people might not consider this squirming, she knew it was as close as Max would ever come. She slowly turned back and looked up at him. "Yes?"

His words sounded almost wracked with pain. "All right. Stick around and I'll…brief you about the case."

Her heartbeat sped up again, but she didn't smile in favor of looking regally triumphant. "Go back to the party, Frank," she told her boss. "I can handle things from here."

"Sure you two won't claw each other's eyes out as soon as I walk out the door?"

She slanted a look in Max's direction. "A tempting notion, but I'll try to resist."

Frank still looked hesitant. And she couldn't blame him—for all he knew, they *would* kill each other. But then he silently departed, pulling the door shut behind him and closing out the gentle sounds of falling rain that had become more audible since she and Max had stopped yelling.

So now they were alone. And everything was quiet, except for the low murmur of music from the stereo, which Max walked over to and turned off, immersing them in a total and intense sort of stillness.

He looked back at her, still standing in the foyer, and their gazes held once more. She wished she could read his eyes, but she'd never gotten very good at it. Still, looking into them reminded her of something she hadn't expected, something that caught her totally off guard—it reminded her of how much she'd *loved* those eyes once upon a time. They were a warm, wrap-around-you shade of brown. And at times, she recalled, they were *more* than warm—they were hot. Sometimes *very* hot. Like when the two of them were sweating and moaning in a glorious symphony of sex.

Uh-oh—she hadn't meant to start thinking about that stuff. She shifted her weight from one stiletto heel to the other and glanced toward the floor.

"Come in and sit down and I'll, uh…go put some clothes on," he said.

"Good idea." In fact, it was the best idea she'd heard since walking into Max Tate's condo. Because the sight of his body had obviously started rekindling some old fires inside her and that wasn't good.

For one thing, they were enemies and she refused to

let herself be attracted to him after the way things had ended between them. And for another, they were about to be partners in a potentially dangerous case that would require all her concentration. So she promised herself that she simply wouldn't think about the sexual aspect of what they'd once shared. She'd blot it right out of her mind. It was the only sensible way to handle the situation.

And now that she had *that* little misunderstanding with herself all cleared up, she could think about this case and what suddenly made it so important to her on a *personal* level—proving to Max Tate that she was a good P.I.

After he'd gone, she moved more deeply into the room, settling on a big leather sofa in the spacious, high-ceilinged room, ready to get geared up for working with him. But then she looked around and saw...his life. His life without *her*.

Okay, so thinking about why the case was important wasn't all that easy at the moment. Her eyes were drawn to pictures on a polished wooden mantle—frames around people who weren't her. Art on the wall he hadn't owned then. Magazines on the table that she'd never known him to have an interest in. In fact, even the furniture was new.

So apparently everything had changed for Max. He'd packed up, gone to Las Vegas, and come back a new man. But it was clear that one thing *hadn't* changed. He still hadn't forgiven her for what happened on the

Carpenter case. As her stomach clenched, she strengthened her vow to prove to him that she could do her job and do it well.

She took another glance around the room—and then it hit her, in a whole new, powerful, horrible way. *Oh God, she was really going to work with Max again. Max,* who had been so much more than just a lover to her, whether or not he knew it. *Max,* whom she'd wanted to build a life with and wake up next to every morning until they were old and gray. This had been the last blow she'd expected today.

But she was an adult. And a professional. She'd told Max she could handle it, so what choice did she have now?

She only hoped she didn't do anything to mess up his career again.

And she hoped she didn't somehow end up falling into bed with him again. Which seemed pretty unlikely considering how much he appeared to despise her. But stranger things had happened, and…oh brother—what had she just gotten herself into?

Chapter Two

LETTING THE TOWEL drop at his feet, Max went to his chest of drawers, pulled out a pair of gray boxer briefs, and stepped into them. Then he yanked a pair of worn blue jeans up from the bedroom floor and put them on, using one hand to swipe a lock of still-wet hair off his forehead.

But an accidental glimpse of himself as he passed by a mirror made him quit going through the hurried motions of getting ready to brief his partner—and come back to reality.

This wasn't just another case. And he wasn't meeting with just another partner.

Kimberly Brandt was sitting in his living room. *Kimberly Brandt* was about to be his partner on the last case of his career.

He rolled his gaze heavenward and let out a mutter. "What could I *possibly* have done to deserve this?"

Hell, he probably should have let her leave with Frank when she wanted to. This was a bad idea—there was just too much bad blood between them to pull this off.

But as he'd told Frank earlier, he really had no choice in the matter. He needed a woman and he needed her by tomorrow morning.

Even so, for the first time since he'd taken this case, he suffered a niggling sense of doubt. Worry. Mistrust. The same mistrust he'd started feeling after the Carpenter case, and the same mistrust that had made him choose to run his business as a one-man operation when he'd moved to Vegas. If you didn't make the mistake of depending upon anyone, they couldn't mess things up for you.

Leaving the West Coast and starting over with his own firm had been the best thing Max had ever done. No one in Vegas had known him or his professional history. He'd performed at peak level for the entire two and a half years he lived there. And he'd discovered that when the gambling mecca's high rollers needed a private investigator, they were happy to loosen their purse strings.

He'd made a killing in just two years. But he'd also gotten tired. And he'd finally admitted to himself that he just didn't like living in the neon desert. So he'd come home with a plan to establish his firm back in L.A., but this time to hire enough good P.I.s that he could run the operation from behind a nice mahogany desk.

And *now...now* he had to worry about this turning into another Carpenter case. Which could ruin his career all over again. His chest tightened.

On another rainy night three years ago, he'd had an appointment with Margaret Carpenter, an elderly lady who walked with a cane and always carried her silver poodle, Lacey, in her free arm. He knew this because he'd been watching her through surveillance equipment in a van near her house for over three weeks. Only Margaret Carpenter hadn't been there when he'd arrived that night. She'd packed up her dog, her belongings, and her stolen money and hadn't been seen since. And it had been all Kimberly's fault.

He and Kimberly had both been employed by the Kessler Agency at the time, the biggest and most prestigious investigation firm in the city. He'd been at the company for nearly ten years and had gradually worked his way up to being the third man in charge. He'd hired Kimberly despite her lack of experience because she'd seemed eager and earnest and willing to learn. He'd had no idea they would soon start dating.

But date they did—quickly making it exclusive. And he'd been…well, damn happy if he was honest with himself. Yet five months into the relationship and six months into her job at Kessler's, Margaret Carpenter had come along.

It had been a pretty simple case initially. Margaret had been stealing money from her son's business and he'd hired Kessler to prove it. The first angle Max had taken had involved sending Kimberly in as a new neighbor. He set her up in a small bungalow next to Margaret's little house and Kimberly forged a relationship with her. The idea had been simply to get the older lady to confess, and hopefully to explain how she'd done it, as well, so that they could track down the physical evidence of her crime.

Max should have known there was trouble, though, when Kimberly told him that she'd met Margaret's son—their client—when he stopped by his mother's house one day and she'd found him rude and brutish. "He's just plain mean to her, Max," she'd said.

"Of course he's mean to her," he'd replied. "He knows she's embezzling his profits."

Kimberly succeeded in getting Margaret to admit that she had over a hundred thousand dollars "saved" and that she was seeking a good investment for it, but she never said where she'd gotten the money. Still, it had been pretty obvious—she didn't work, lived meagerly, and had access to her son's accounts, a mistake of him being too trusting when opening his construction business years earlier as a young man.

The next angle they'd planned to take was to send Max in as a friend of Kimberly's, a real estate broker who could help Margaret invest her cash. He would ask how much money she had and tell her he needed more, quickly, for a sure-thing investment. Even if they couldn't get a confession from her, they'd watch the accounts for the amount he requested.

But by the time he got there that night, the house was dark and Margaret Carpenter was on her way into hiding. Because, unbeknownst to him, Kimberly had broken all the rules of ethics by telling Margaret who they were and what her son suspected.

He remembered all too clearly the day both of them had been called into Dean Kessler's office. Max had found out Kimberly was responsible for Margaret's departure just moments before—when she'd told him herself, obviously sensing why Kessler had called the meeting.

Kessler had first fired Kimberly, after furiously pointing out that they all could have lost their licenses over this kind of behavior.

And then Kessler fired him, too.

He hadn't seen it coming—he'd thought he was only involved as Kimberly's direct superior—and having just found out what she'd done had been upsetting *enough*. Instead Kessler had held him entirely responsible for the whole damn debacle. "You hired her. And you put her on this case. And you also got sloppy, Max."

"Sloppy?" He'd leaned forward, eyebrows raised.

"This is what happens when you start thinking more about what's under your employee's skirt than about her work. You lose your judgment and she botches the job."

Then Kessler had walked out of his own office, leaving them both alone. And Max had sunk more deeply into the chair where he sat, trying to wrap his head around the fact that he'd just lost everything he'd worked to build for the previous ten years. He was dumbfounded that it could be taken from him that quickly. Not to mention indignant, resentful, and downright angry.

Slowly, he'd turned his head to look at Kimberly—the woman who'd done this to him. Tears stained her cheeks as their eyes met, and her voice came out whispery sad. "I suppose it's too late to say I'm sorry."

Sorry? He'd just lost his whole career. Sorry didn't begin to cover it. "Too late," he'd said. "And too damn little."

She'd swallowed visibly and they'd simply sat staring at each other for a long, painful moment. And then she'd stood up and walked out. Out of the office. And out of his life.

He hadn't seen her again until he'd exited the shower ten minutes ago and found her standing in his foyer, rainwater dripping from the hem of her short blue dress and the tips of her wavy hair, a smug sassiness he didn't remember from before now overflowing from her.

She was everything he'd asked Frank for. Smart. A good actress. And God knew she was a pleasure to look at.

But there'd been one thing he'd left out of his description of the perfect lady partner when he'd talked to Frank. Trustworthiness. She'd proven to him three years ago that she couldn't be counted on to maintain her loyalty or finish a job. She'd cost him everything.

And now they were supposed to work together?

KIMBERLY CROSSED AND uncrossed her legs. Then she firmly crossed her arms under her breasts. What the hell was taking him so long? First he'd kept her waiting at the door, now in his living room. How long did it take a man to get dressed?

Finally, she released a sharp sigh of irritation and leaned forward on the couch. "Um, excuse me in there? Those clothes you went to put on? Are you weaving the fabric yourself or—?"

She flinched when he exited the bedroom and walked toward her down the hardwood hall in bare feet. The flinch came because his chest was also bare, and his jeans were pleasantly low-slung and snug in all the right places. Or maybe those were actually—on second thought—the wrong places. Oh my. She leaned back into the couch, trying to pretend she hadn't just had a spasm at the very sight of him.

"You bellowed?" he asked, widening his dark eyes in a way that might have struck her as...warm, or maybe even sultry, if it hadn't been coupled with sarcasm.

"I just wanted to make sure you hadn't dozed off or something." She uncrossed her legs, then recrossed them the other way. "And if this is going to take a while, shouldn't you call Julie and change your plans?" Oh drat—she'd tried to resist saying that last part, but it had slipped out anyway. Despite herself, she wanted to know who Julie was.

But all she got for her efforts was yet another of Max's classic dry looks as he shoved a lock of dark hair from his forehead. "Don't worry, Brandt. I'm completely capable of handling my own affairs."

The response cut her to the quick. Although she didn't know what bothered her more—the allusion she knew he was making to the Carpenter case and the underlying suggestion that she wasn't capable of handling *anything*, or hearing him say the word *affairs* and thinking of him having them—not with her anymore, but with other women. With this, this *Julie* person.

However, she quickly deduced that the allusion to that last case they'd worked on ate at her the most. Because she still suffered the compulsion to try explaining to him why she'd done what she'd done that night. "Believe it or not, Tate, I'm capable, too. More than capable. And as for the Carpenter case—"

He held up his hand. "Stop."

She snapped her response. "Why?"

Settling in a leather chair across from her, he narrowed his gaze on her. "Because if this is going to work, we need to push our bad feelings for each other aside and stick to the case."

"That's a spiffy plan, Tate, but if you'd just let me tell you my side of things, I'm sure we'd both—"

"Nope," he cut her off. "The past is in the past and I have no desire to dredge it back up. That's how it has to be if we're going to work together."

She released a bitter sigh. She should have known better. After all, she'd tried to explain outside Kessler's office that day, but he hadn't let her then, either. He'd just kept saying, "You told her *what*?" as he glared at her with disbelieving eyes. And then Kessler had called them in and that had been the end of it. He wouldn't let her explain then, and he still wouldn't let her explain now. "Fine," she bit off.

"Now, about the case."

She shifted on the couch, trying to relax and get into a professional frame of mind. "I'm listening."

"The guy we're after is Carlo Coletti. Carlo makes a pastime of robbing wealthy wives of their expensive jewelry."

"How does he go about it?"

"He hangs out in upscale drinking establishments until he can befriend some rich guy and cling onto him. He makes a point of getting the guy to show him a picture of his wife—who, as far as I can tell, has to be a knockout in order to get Coletti interested—and then he ingratiates himself into the couple's lives. After that, he seduces the wife and steals her jewelry in the process."

She tilted her head. He'd obviously glossed over some details. "Fill in the gaps, Tate."

"Well, in my client's case, the guy seduced her and charmed the jewelry away from her. Told her it turned him on to make love to a woman decked out in diamonds. She went to her safe, put on every diamond necklace and bracelet she owned, slept with the guy, then woke up hours later naked of even the jewels."

Kimberly was beginning to think she got the picture here. "So, it's more than just money for this guy. He's after the thrills, too."

Max gave a short nod. "Would seem that way. Another thing pointing in that direction is the fact that he *could* just pick up rich *single* women. But he only goes for couples. He seems to like seducing the wife away from her wealthy husband. The scam tears the victims apart. In addition to robbing my client, he broke up her marriage, too."

"You said *victims*. So there are other known victims besides your client?"

"I've talked with four."

"And if everyone knows what happened, and if this guy is so easy to find, why isn't he behind bars?"

Max offered a wry smile. "That's the tricky part. Police have checked him out, held him on suspicion—and he even went to trial once. But he says he didn't do it and no one can prove anything. Claims he seduces the wives, but that's it—no jewelry. To top it off, the guy lives in a dumpy apartment near Venice. It's been searched over and over and the police never turn up anything. The most valuable things in this guy's possession are his car and the clothes on his back, which make him fit in with the rich set well enough at a glance. But whatever he's doing with the jewels, he's covering his tracks and keeping it quiet. He's stolen over three million dollars' worth from the four women I've spoken to, yet there's not a shred of evidence."

"And that's where we come in."

"Right. Tomorrow morning you and I move into a mansion in Beverly Hills, borrowed from a well-off friend of my client's, a studio bigwig who's out of town for the next month. Tomorrow night, Carlo Coletti joins us for dinner and the party begins."

"One question," she asked. "If you didn't even know who your wife was going to be, you obviously couldn't show the jerk her picture. How'd you reel him in without it?"

Their eyes met. "I assured him that my wife was the most beautiful, vibrant, sexy, sultry woman he'd ever have the pleasure of meeting."

Is she? She wanted to ask, but held her tongue. His gaze on her, saying those words, made her throat tighten and the juncture between her thighs tingle.

So that was when she rose from the couch, suddenly ready to end the meeting. "Is there anything else I need to know?"

He stood up, as well. "Nothing I can't fill you in on tomorrow. But be prepared—the guy's gonna be all over you as soon as he gets one look. And if you have any sexy clothes, bring 'em—we want to paint you as...not unwilling."

"Sexy clothes," she murmured. But she was still stuck on the first thing he'd said. *The guy's gonna be all over you.*

Ugh. *Wrong guy.*

Yet then she cursed herself. *Damn it, quit thinking about Max like that.*

"Like what you're wearing right now," he added.

She blinked, a little confused—then she glanced down, unaware that the simple blue sheathe qualified as sexy. "This?"

He nodded. "I saw you from the back at Frank's party. Even without seeing your face, you were easily the hottest woman in the room."

Despite the suggestive words, his voice held zero emotion. So as the warmth of a blush attack her cheeks, she turned away. She padded toward the mantle and studied the pictures there, attempting to block out the increased fluttering sensations that rippled through her body.

Which one might be Julie?

Though...a closer look revealed that *none of them* could be. She found two pictures of his parents—an older one and another more recent, and a picture of Max and his three brothers taken long before she'd known him. Still, the exercise hadn't succeeded in distracting her enough—every part of her body hummed with awareness of his presence and what he'd just said.

"I'll get you a cab," he announced behind her. But she still didn't turn around. She didn't want him to see how his words had affected her. Even if she kept hearing them over and over again. *You were easily the hottest woman in the room.*

A few long minutes later, the beep of a horn from outside announced the taxi's arrival, something that was more than welcome. She grabbed up her purse and shawl, then moved briskly to Max's front door, whisking it open to let in the sound of the rain and a glimpse of the shiny black street.

"Give some thought to your part and establish a character," he told her before she could exit.

The sound of his voice stopped her—and she turned to peer back at him, unable to resist a last look at this man she'd thought she'd never see again. Her heart ached a bit—at the sight of him, and at the memories of what they once had.

"I'll be by to pick you up at ten tomorrow morning," he told her. "And after that, we'll be as good as married."

Chapter Three

IT WAS STRANGE to be driving to Kimberly's apartment after all this time. Strange that he made each turn on the route almost without thinking—like it was still a natural place for him to go. Just the same, he still couldn't get over the fact that the woman Frank had partnered him with was her.

Max tried to quit seeing all the emotions that had flashed through her eyes last night, but she'd always been lousy at hiding that kind of thing. His stomach clenched slightly recalling her hurt look when he'd refused to let her give her version of the Carpenter case.

But there was a reason for that: It didn't matter. No matter what she said, her actions remained a breach of ethics. No matter what she said, it would never be enough to make up for costing him his position at the company where he'd spent his entire adult life building a career.

Knowing that no answer would ever satisfy him had made it easier to go to Vegas. And besides, she'd walked away. She'd gotten up and walked out of Kessler's office without looking back. It had appeared that things were finished. That they had to be.

He hadn't liked or wanted any of it—not professionally, not personally. But it had seemed that the smart thing to do was to move on with his life and salvage what had been left of his career. And the smart thing to do *now* was not to think about the past, as he'd told her last night. Looking back wouldn't do either of them any good.

After parking outside her building, he stepped out into one of the first truly hot days of summer. Sun beat down from a cloudless sky, the only reprieve a gentle breeze that whispered through the trees lining the mid-city sidewalk. He liked days like this—hot and bright—better than the softer days of a California spring or fall. He liked extremes, always had. That's how he'd ended up being a P.I.

Well, the next few days should definitely be extreme enough. And admittedly, he'd feel better if he were working with anyone else besides Kimberly Brandt, but he couldn't keep dwelling on that—he had to get on with the business of catching Carlo Coletti.

When he knocked, she came to the door in faded jeans and a fitted Mickey Mouse T-shirt. He knew it was ludicrous, but for some reason he'd been expecting to see her in that blue dress again. Her hair, which had been elegantly styled last night, today fell around her face in tousled waves, and her blue jeans looked soft and comfortable above bare feet.

He missed the obvious attributes of the dress immediately—she looked much plainer than last night—yet a rivulet of warmth trickled through him when he least anticipated it. Maybe like this, she reminded him of lazy afternoons spent driving nowhere with the top down, or of rainy days spent on the couch watching old movies and eating pizza between kisses.

Geez, shake it off, Tate. He'd gotten lost there for a minute, but he was back now.

He forced himself to meet her eyes—although just as quickly, she lowered her gaze to her own shirt. "What the hell are you staring at?"

Damn—he'd been looking her up and down like a woman who wore lingerie instead of a T-shirt and jeans. He gave his head a light shake. "Nothing."

"Look," she said belligerently, "if I was supposed to be dressed in character already, you should have mentioned it."

He pushed past her into the apartment, not inclined to explain himself. "What you're wearing is fine for now. Where's your stuff?" He glanced around the room, at the familiar clutter and the antique furniture she liked, and spotted it himself—a garment bag tossed across the couch and a rolling suitcase on the floor.

"It's right there—"

But he had already picked them both up and was headed for the door. "Come on—let's get moving."

"If we're in a race, Tate, I should probably at least put on some shoes, don't you think?"

He stopped and looked back at her from the hallway outside the door, unamused. "Hurry up," he told her.

The way he saw it, he didn't have time to wait on her, and he didn't have time to think about past days spent with her, either. There was a job to be done and the sooner it was over the better—then he could get on with his life.

As Max's Porsche hugged the curves of the road that led from Kimberly's apartment toward Beverly Hills, she watched him driving from the corner of her eye. His strong hands gripped the wheel tightly, but he let his long, sturdy body lean back in the seat like a man completely comfortable with himself. That was Max, she thought. He'd never lacked confidence.

"Nice day, huh?" she asked.

"Yeah." Short and clipped.

Yep, he had plenty of confidence, but manners had never been his strong suit.

She tried again a few minutes later, asking how his parents were doing. "Fine," he replied, eyes glued on the road.

All right, she got the hint. He wasn't disposed to making small talk.

And it was probably just as well. After all, they weren't buddies. They weren't pals. They were two people doing a job together. That was all.

"You should put on your seatbelt," she told him anyway. She'd always been big on seatbelts and noticed when people weren't wearing them.

But he simply cast her an annoyed look in reply.

"It's the law," she pointed out. "And besides, the way you drive, you may need it. Put it on."

After an anoyed sigh, he reached over his shoulder for the belt, muttering something below his breath.

"What?" she snapped. "I couldn't quite hear you."

"I was just saying," he answered, louder and clearly irritated, "that I forgot what a seatbelt fanatic you are."

She rolled her eyes and crossed her arms, then turned to peer out the window.

"We should probably talk about our covers," he said then, surprising her with even that bit of conversation—and spoken in an almost cordial tone, too.

She nodded. "All right."

He gave her a short glance, then looked back to the road. "We'll keep our first names and my last one, making you Kimberly Tate."

She nodded again, wishing she didn't like the sound of that so much. This wasn't helpful for her freshly reactivated plan of not thinking about him that way.

"I'm a stockbroker—I work for Finch and Company downtown, and I bring home two and a half mil a year. I've been with the company for ten years and was made partner after five. I'm a Los Angeles native and so are you. We met in college at UCLA. As for our families, should it come up, we'll keep them as they are—same names, same backgrounds, same everything—it'll be less to remember."

"What about me?" she asked.

"What *about* you?"

"What do *I* do?"

"You sit at home all day and be rich. You bask in luxury."

Oh. Hmm. What a drag that sounded like. Until an idea hit her. "Maybe I'm bored with you."

He turned to glare at her.

"Tate, the road!"

As he turned his eyes back to driving, she said, "See what I mean about the seatbelt?"

When he ignored her, she went on. "Anyway, I was thinking about why I would be interested in sleeping with this guy. So maybe it's because I'm bored. Bored with my life of leisure. Bored with you."

"Not possible."

Like last night when he'd told her how hot she was, his voice came without inflection. And she thought of arguing that it certainly *was* possible in the given scenario.

But then she remembered the way Max made love.

Polite he wasn't, but generous in bed—yes. He put his whole self, his whole soul, into the act.

And she didn't know if he was thinking about the same thing, too—about the way they used to do it for hours until they were both exhausted and drenched in sweat and completely sated—but all things considered, she decided it would be simpler not to argue. "Okay then, if that's not the problem, why *would* I consider sleeping with this guy?"

"Maybe you're getting back at me."

"What did you do?"

"Cheated on you."

"You wouldn't," she gasped, fearful it sounded more like a jealous plea than a statement. Asinine thoughts of the mysterious Julie came to mind.

"Why not?"

She took a deep breath as something slightly wicked, and slightly seductive, came oozing up from inside her. "Wait until you see me in the dress I'm wearing to dinner tonight, Tate," she told him. "Trust me. You wouldn't."

"OH MY GOD."

Max's car had just emerged from a grove of billowing storybook trees on the winding drive that led to their borrowed mansion. The home before them boasted two incredibly tall columns that stretched from the expansive front porch to an arch at the top of the third story. Part brick, part white stucco, and nestled deep in the wooded hills, it made Kimberly think of a fairytale paradise.

"Get used to it," he told her as she continued to gape. The car came to a halt in the circular drive that fronted the mansion and she stumbled out, still taking in the splendor of it all. "You live here, you know. You can't seem too amazed by anything."

"I've got all day to work on that," she told him. "But for now, I can't help it—I'm pretty amazed."

"There's a pool. Did you bring a suit?"

She glanced over her shoulder and gave a short nod, then returned her gaze to the house. She'd figured no decent mansion would be caught dead without a pool. Now that she saw the place, she was surprised it didn't have two or three.

"What's it like?"

She finally turned to give him her full attention. "What's what like?"

"Your swimsuit."

Despite the suggestion, she knew why he was asking. It had nothing to do with *him*. It had to do with their job. "Yes, it's a bikini. Our houseguest should love it."

He nodded in reply, then started getting her stuff from the car—but not before she thought she detected an unexpected glimmer of interest twinkling in his eyes. So maybe it *wasn't* just a business question. Her pulse raced with the idea that he might still be attracted to her.

But damn it, why did she even care? She stomped her foot on the brick driveway to punctuate her annoyance with herself. *She was here to arouse the bad guy, not Max.*

Still, could she help it if Max got aroused, too? After all, she was only doing her job.

Not that arousal meant romance—often the two weren't even connected, but…she couldn't stop her mind from meandering in that direction.

"Something wrong?"

She peered up with innocent eyes as Max rounded the car with her bags. "No. Why?"

"I thought you were stepping on a bug or something." He looked toward the flip-flop adorned foot she'd just stomped.

But Max wasn't the only one who could avoid unwanted conversations. "Let's go inside," she said. "I want to look around." Then she rushed ahead toward the door.

BEYOND THE FOYER, lined with Mexican tile, the immense house stretched in all directions. A bright, spacious living room with a vaulted ceiling and huge picture windows that looked out on the pool area and view beyond caught Kimberly's eye straight ahead and stretching to the right. To the left rested a crisp white kitchen with a large cooking island and a breakfast nook with another picture window.

Awed, she roamed the length of the nearest hallway, discovering an elegant dining room filled with massive furniture, Renaissance art gracing the walls. She next happened upon an office connected to a library, a billiards room, and an extravagant bathroom big enough to house a small family. After which she strolled through a door into a five-car garage, a couple of the spots empty—however, a gray Mercedes, a late model Corvette in red, and a vintage green Jaguar convertible from the 1940s rested neatly in the other spaces.

Returning on the route she'd traveled, she found Max waiting for her at the bottom of a curved staircase she'd glimpsed off the foyer, looking annoyed. "Do you mind?" he muttered.

"Do I mind what?" she asked cheerfully, still quite taken with the house.

"Not wandering off when I'm standing here waiting for you. This thing weighs a ton." He motioned to the suitcase clutched in his right fist.

Feeling surprisingly merry now, she took the garment bag from his other hand. "Shoes," she explained of the suitcase. "Lots of them. And it has wheels, you know, so you don't have to stand there holding it and acting like such an irritated he-man about it." Then she passed him on the stairs, in awe of the spectacular home she would call her own for the next couple of days.

Once upstairs, she dragged her garment bag on another quick exploratory excursion—this time finding bedroom after bedroom, each designed with its own extravagant style. None of the lavish rooms appeared lived in, so she suspected they were all guestrooms.

When she glanced over her shoulder to see Max, he still looked annoyed at her amazement. But she didn't care. This place was *too* fabulous, and if he was smart, he'd let her get the wonderment out of her system before their guest arrived later.

In the meantime, she was ready to unload the garment bag. "Um, where is our—"

"That way." He pointed to the end of the hall she

hadn't yet approached, and she headed in that direction, instantly glad he hadn't let her finish the sentence. She was overwhelmed enough at the moment without being forced to start thinking about their sleeping arrangements.

She burst through the double doors to the master suite and released a heartfelt gasp, completely thunderstruck. Four thick, polished wood posts emerged from the enormous bed with beams connecting them at the top to create a canopy effect, from which a wide swath of filmy white fabric cascaded like a chiffon waterfall. Underneath, the bed was adorned with more throw pillows than she'd ever seen in one place. The cathedral ceiling featured skylights, and a small stone fireplace graced one corner of the room where two stylish easy chairs set on either side of a low marble table.

She flung her garment bag on the bed and spun to face Max, who lingered in the doorway. "Have you seen this? It's gorgeous!"

But it would seem that Max never smiled anymore. "That it is," he agreed dryly, stepping into the room and lowering her suitcase to the floor. "You'll also find a huge master bath with a tub set in marble and matching rainfall shower, and a walk-in closet big enough to be a bedroom. But Brandt, *you own all this stuff.* So it's no big deal, remember? Get used to it."

Sheesh—did he have to take all the fun out of *everything*? "Relax," she snipped at him. "I *will* get used to it. And I'll know every inch of it by heart before tonight.

But for now, is it so horrible for you to let me enjoy it for a minute?"

"I'm not paying you to enjoy anything. I'm paying you to do what you're supposed to do. Think you can handle that?"

She turned to face him, speechless, the wind knocked out of her buoyant sails. But she didn't need to say anything anyway—they both knew what he was talking about. "Then I guess we'd better get to work," she finally replied in her most mocking tone.

But when would she learn? A little mocking never daunted Max. "Yes. We'd better."

He then broke the tension—even if she was the only one feeling it—by moving straight into showing her the dresser drawers that had been cleared for her, as well as closet space for her clothes. It felt a little strange to be using someone else's closet, with all their stuff still inside, but she took it in stride. And she tried to hide her astonishment at the size of the massive dream closet, too, lest Max think she was having too good a time on the job.

"Most importantly," he told her as they exited the so-called closet back into the bedroom, "is this." He lifted a painting from the wall and revealed a safe. "The combination is simple. Thirty, thirty-one, thirty-two." Even simpler to remember, Kimberly thought, since she'd just turned thirty-one, right in the middle.

She watched as Max spun the knob on the lock three times, then opened the safe door and pulled out a round black velvet box that measured at least a foot in diameter. After he pushed it into her hands, she reached down to lift the lid.

"What's in—oh!" It was mostly diamonds, with a few emeralds and sapphires mixed in. She gaped at the jewels, then raked her hand through them to scoop up necklaces and bracelets that dripped like streams of shimmering water through her fingers.

"Fake, of course," Max pointed out.

She'd figured that. But they were still beautiful. "What if our guy's a jewelry expert?"

"Good question," he said. And the way things were going, she was surprised he'd concede something even as small as that. "But they're not *cheap* fake. They're as good as fake gets, supplied by my client. Unless Carlo has a jeweler's loop in his pocket, he won't be able to tell. Besides, his thefts are sudden and quick—he doesn't have time to analyze the goods. So we should be fine on that count."

She closed the box and handed it back to Max, who returned it to the safe and locked the door. "Practice opening the safe later," he told her, "and familiarize yourself with the jewelry so you'll know how all the clasps work and that sort of thing."

She nodded, then turned toward the garment bags that lay on the bed.

On the bed that they would supposedly...*share*?

She guessed it was time to bite the bullet, act professional, and ask him just what his plans were for that.

"Where will...um, everyone sleep?" She posed the question casually, with her back to him.

"Everyone?"

"Well, you and me. And Carlo," she added, turning to face him. "And while we're on the subject, just why does he think you've invited him here?"

"Stocks," Max answered confidently. "Carlo claims he wants to learn about the stock market and I'm just the guy to teach him."

"You are?"

"I know enough to fake it. When he expressed an interest, I suggested we get together one evening. I'd been hanging out with him for a few nights by then, so it didn't seem odd to invite him to dinner."

"And why does he think he's spending the night?"

"He doesn't necessarily, yet. But according to all the victims I've talked with, he gets chummy fast and then finds a way to prod the invitation."

She nodded, then realized she'd never let Max answer her original question. Her chest tightened as she brought it back up. "So, about the sleeping arrangements ..."

"Carlo will take one of the guestrooms," he said.

Okay, get to the important part already. But when he didn't launch right into that, she heard herself talking, rushing to fill the empty space. "I'm guessing you and I will pretend to sleep here—" she pointed to the bed, "—but that one of us will really take another bedroom after lights are out."

Yet Max gave his head a decisive shake. "No way,

Brandt. Too easy to get caught and it would look suspicious as hell. Some things you can't pretend—so you and I will definitely be sharing this bed."

Chapter Four

SHE LOOKED BACK and forth between him and the bed, half surprised at his answer, and half surprised that she actually thought it sounded like such an awful idea. After all, despite the front she was putting up, in her heart of hearts, she'd almost already admitted to herself that the idea of sleeping next to Max turned her insides to jelly, no matter how much he disliked her.

Now, however, faced with doing just that, her muscles tensed and her stomach churned. And if it was something she really wanted, would it make her feel sick like this? So maybe she really *was* capable of not thinking of Max that way.

But she could ponder that later—right now she had to deal with the matter at hand. "Do you think that's...appropriate?"

"Not particularly," he said. "But husbands and wives generally sleep together. Sleeping apart wouldn't do much to uphold our cover."

"We could make it look like we're having a fight. That might make me seem like easier prey."

He shook his head, appearing as decisive as ever. "That's just it—Carlo doesn't want easy prey. Or at least not *that* easy. He gets off on seducing the otherwise loving wife from her husband. He wants to be the choice, not the fallback position."

Pulling in her breath, she tried again. "Well, what was wrong with my first idea? The one where we act like we're turning in together and then later you sneak out and sleep somewhere else." She still thought it was a pretty good suggestion. Of course, maybe that was because she felt desperate and didn't have any other ones.

Yet it only brought another headshake. "He might get up in the night and realize we aren't together, that's what. What if he were to look into the room while we're sleeping or something?"

She grimaced. "You think that's possible?"

"How would I know? The guy's a creep. Anything's possible. Which reminds me, we need to talk about actually nailing this jerk."

She let out a sigh she hoped Max didn't see. It would seem the matter was settled, whether she liked it or not—so onto the next item of business. Lowering herself onto the ornate bed, she said, "I'm listening."

"The only thing Carlo's seductions have in common," Max said, "is that he moves in for the kill when the husband's not home, and he ends up getting out of the house with jewelry—usually without the woman's knowledge. In one case, the wife went to take a shower after they'd had sex—taking off her jewelry beforehand—and when she came back, he was gone, along with the gems. And like I told you before, he actually took the jewelry off *my* client while she was sleeping. Another woman chose to refuse his advances—which is what will happen with you. She ran out of the room, at which point Carlo wiped her dresser clean of all the jewels other than what she was wearing, then took off."

"So I'll refuse his advances—but where will *you* be?"

"This is going to be a carefully orchestrated operation, Brandt. A while after we've all gone to bed, I'll pretend I got an urgent call and need to leave for a work emergency—and I'll wake Carlo to let him know. I'll also mention that you have trouble sleeping when I'm away. I won't really take off, though—I'll actually be in the closet," he said, motioning to it. "Then you'll invite him into the bedroom to keep you company, or to see the view from the balcony or something—unless he just shows up on his own first, which is likely."

At this, she rose from the bed and padded over to check out said view. The balcony overlooked an expansive pool and, beyond that, a vast tree-filled valley that stretched for miles, dotted with only other mansions and estates.

"I'll be videotaping the theft," Max continued, "and I'll also be there just in case you have any trouble fending the guy off. Hopefully, he'll back off easily but still use the opportunity to swipe the jewelry anyway."

Kimberly nodded. Sounded pretty straightforward.

"Any questions, Brandt?"

"None."

"All right then. I'll give you a few minutes to unpack your stuff." And that quickly, he was out the door and she was alone in this fabulous room where a crime would soon take place. And where she and Max would soon share a bed. Which bothered her even more as she thought about it, actually making her stomach clench. She didn't *want* to sleep next to Max tonight. Or any other night.

She felt better knowing that—knowing that whatever she'd been feeling around him last night and this morning had apparently faded. But she *didn't* feel better knowing that they were going to sleep in this bed together. Something about it actually made her skin crawl.

Only…now that she thought about it, maybe Max hadn't thought through that part as clearly as he acted like. After all, it sounded like they would only pretend to go to bed for a little while—with, she presumed, the goal of placing her in the bedroom with the jewels when Max pretended to depart, making it easy for the thief. And if it all went as planned, the theft would take place, Carlo would be long gone, and then sleeping arrangements wouldn't matter. In fact, they might end up being awake all night anyway, going to the client or the police with the tape and ultimately heading home before morning. She supposed a lot of this would be left up to happenstance and timing. But the realization made it easier to move past the issue of sharing a bed with Max onto more productive things.

Unpacking didn't take long. She added her array of sexy dresses to the already filled closet, put her toiletries in the bathroom, and stuck her bikini and lacy undies in the drawers provided. She had no intention of letting Carlo Coletti see her in anything lacy, of course, but it had seemed like a good thing to have around just in case he did something gross like went through her drawers. Besides, the character of Mrs. Max Tate, whom she would become this evening, didn't wear cotton panties like Kimberly mostly did. Only the most luxurious of fabrics for Kimberly Tate, stockbroker's wife and femme fatale.

Max had explained to her already that the rest of the house was completely furnished and stocked with food, drink, and everything else people needed to live. Before the day was through, she'd have to tour it carefully and find out the little things—where they kept the bath towels, what kind of food was on hand, how the alarm system worked. She'd have to make sure it seemed like she and Max really lived there.

Of course, that was only part of it. They had to do more than live there—they had to convince Carlo Coletti that they were married. Had Max really thought about that? She wandered back to the bed and let herself plop down on it to stare up at the vaulted ceiling. Perhaps she should address the question with him, but it seemed a touchy subject. She didn't want to imply that they should or shouldn't do any specific married-seeming things in front of Carlo Coletti. Physical things, for instance. Still, wouldn't they have to? The thought made her shiver, just like when she thought of sharing this bed with him. But she guessed she had no choice but to cross that bridge when she came to it.

And maybe Max *did* have a plan. Maybe he was going to portray himself as one of those unaffectionate husbands who took their wives for granted and never paid them any attention. Of course, maybe that wouldn't work if Coletti was set on tearing apart a happy couple. But as cold as Max was acting to her, the neglectful husband would be an easy role for him to take on.

He seemed to think he was the only one of them who had suffered any losses because of the Carpenter case. He blamed her for everything, though—so of course he wouldn't be sitting around thinking about how *her* life had been affected. She'd lost her job, which she'd loved, and she'd lost *him*, whom she'd also loved, all in one fell swoop. Not to mention that at the time she'd also been dealing with the very fresh news that her mother had cancer.

Two months of depression later, she'd pulled herself together enough to take a job with another company. The guy she'd worked for, though, wasn't as good as Max, and business was bad. When the agency finally folded just over a year ago, she'd signed on with Frank.

She'd recovered from the blows she'd taken during that period, but she considered it the blackest spot of her entire past, for reasons both professional and personal.

Oh sure, she'd made mistakes under Max's tutelage, but she'd never completely screwed up a case before that. And until then, she'd never been fired from a job in her life.

Worse yet, his way of handling the situation had shown her that he obviously hadn't cared for her very much. Yes, she'd been the one to walk out of that office. But he'd been the one who didn't stop her. And then he'd gone to Las Vegas, just like that.

Only then had she come to the conclusion that what they'd shared had been one-sided. Not sexually—she knew that. But in other ways. Emotional ways. It had made her glad she'd never said the words that had lingered on the tip of her tongue whenever they were together—*I love you*. And if any shred of doubt about how he felt had been left dangling in the back of her mind, seeing him—first last night and then again today—had killed it off entirely. It was clear she'd been nothing to him.

But that's okay. She pushed down an old familiar hurt as it bolted through her *That's okay because you don't even want to share a bed with him. You don't want to be close to him.* Last night and this morning, that was like shell-shock or something. But the fact was—she was *over* Max. Completely. And for good. As of right now, he was nothing to her, either.

MAX LAY ON the plush leather couch in the big family

room watching TV—trying to take it easy in the last few hours before the show began, and also trying to get acclimated and feel as if this place, this life, was *his*. Meanwhile, his weekend wife was in the kitchen digging through drawers and cabinets, getting familiar with things. Personally, he thought she was overdoing it, but he wasn't going to chastise her. It couldn't hurt for her to know where they kept stuff.

He didn't know why he'd made that crack earlier—the one about her handling the job. He'd told himself this morning that he had to quit that crap if they were going to work together with any success, but it had leaked out like air escaping a punctured balloon.

Three years hadn't healed his mistrust of her. This was going to be hard, perhaps the hardest case of his career—and now it was being made even harder, not only by his fears of her screwing up or letting him down, but also because he had to own up to the fact that he was still attracted to her. Which he'd have to forget or ignore or something. It was like he'd told Frank last night. If he wanted sex, he could get it. He certainly wouldn't attempt to get that or anything else from the woman who had betrayed him.

"Oh my God, we have caviar!"

Her voice sounded from somewhere in the kitchen behind him and he worked to hold in even the hint of a smile—whether she could see him or not. He couldn't start going soft on her. But that's what he remembered about Kimberly. How fascinated she could be by the world. How in awe.

Maybe that was why he'd given her such a hard time over her wonder regarding the house—maybe he hadn't wanted to be reminded of *her*, and of *him*, of them *together*. And maybe that was why he'd thought this morning of those simple, easy times with her, those T-shirt and jeans times.

He knew they'd done other things, too—gone out to dinner, to plays, to clubs—but she could find an unmitigated joy just in eating ice cream or watching the rain fall. She wasn't like that *all* the time—when she was working, she was strictly business. But when work was done, she took the playing of life pretty seriously, and he'd liked that.

She came rushing into the room in a flurry then, cutting into his thoughts and stirring up a small breeze. "Tate, I just thought of something!"

"What's that?"

"Dinner! Am I supposed to be cooking this dinner? Because if I am, what am I making? And how am I making it? I mean, I cook—you know I cook—but I don't...*cook*. Not anything fancy. So...?"

He hesitated, feeling devilish for no reason and having no luck in pushing it down. "I thought maybe you'd learned, taken lessons or something."

She widened her eyes in what was obviously sheer horror. "Why on earth would you think that?"

"Well, you're here all day alone, and bored, or so you said. I thought maybe you'd taken up a hobby."

He thought it obvious that he was only kidding, but she looked all the more horrified. And maybe that was understandable—this was the first time he'd done anything even remotely light-hearted since laying eyes on her.

And actually, that was a bad idea. Hadn't he just told himself not to go soft on her? There would be enough of that once they assumed their roles as husband and wife.

"Tate, if you were going to write things like that into my character, you could've at least warned me and I'd have studied a cookbook last night or something. Now, the way I see it is—you were right and I'm *not* bored. And I've been far too busy eating bonbons and lounging around in diamonds to cook anything at all. Which leaves one question. What are we going to do about dinner?"

This time he made sure to keep his face expressionless. It was much safer not to let her know he was even mildly entertained by anything she did. "Don't worry. I have a chef coming at five-thirty. She'll serve us at seven, then clean up the mess when we're through."

Kimberly let out a sigh of relief. "A chef. That's good." Yet then she was suddenly looking around, no longer in awe, but as if something terrible had just struck her. "You know, Tate, this is a big place. Shouldn't we have housekeepers or something? Shouldn't we have a *full-time* chef?"

"Already thought of that," he said, remaining emotionless. "I'll just mention to Carlo that our housekeeper, who doubles as our chef, asked for the weekend off. So when she leaves after dinner, it won't seem weird."

"Ah," she said, nodding. "Okay—that'll work."

"Of course it will," he answered absently. And from his peripheral vision, he saw her standing there watching him watch TV, since he'd made a point of returning his attention to it already. And maybe she was waiting for him to say something more, keep this merry little conversation going, but nope—that was a bad idea. Conversation over.

This will be simple as long as you remember the rules. No more Mr. Nice Guy.

SCENTS OF SOMETHING succulent met Kimberly's nose as she moved delicately down the stairway in five-inch heels. But she couldn't look forward to dinner, or enjoy her surroundings, or even anticipate the thrill of satisfaction in the job that was about to begin. Her chest felt tight and her throat did, too. And the butterflies that had invaded her stomach while she dressed had suddenly fled the scene—because apparently someone was releasing hand grenades in there now.

She wasn't nervous about the job.

She wasn't nervous about Carlo Coletti.

She was nervous about Max. About Max seeing her.

Odd, for a second there earlier, when they'd been discussing the whole dinner thing, she'd thought she'd sensed something new in him—something fresh and almost friendly. A hint of a smile and maybe even a soft tone. But things had changed suddenly and quickly as he'd put his typical wall up between them and she'd been forced to change her opinion. Max, friendly? Nope, she'd clearly been imagining things. Now she had to wonder all the more how things would be between them as they progressed into the charade part of this case, and as she became his "wife."

At the bottom of the stairs she approached a mosaic-framed mirror that reflected her image from head to toe. Her hair was bunched up on top of her head, tiny wisps of it falling over her cheeks and nape. Along with a "wedding ring" pilfered from the black box upstairs, she wore a pair of fake diamond earrings that dangled and sometimes tickled her neck, and a thin fake diamond necklace that she thought of as a sort of teaser for their guest.

But the real event was clearly taking place *below* her neck. The dress was slinky and black and short and hugged her every curve. Tiny straps held up the low-cut bodice, which was built for cleavage and definitely delivered. She was pretty sure she'd been a size smaller when she'd bought this dress. And it had looked fine on her then, hanging looser and more comfortably around her. But now—well, she finally understood how it was *meant* to fit. She barely recognized herself. And she couldn't help wondering how Max would react to her like this.

She tried to tell herself that her anxiety was because

she wanted to please him as an employee wishes to please a boss, that she wanted him to think she was the perfect woman for this job. But it was more than that. She'd tried to tell herself ever since she'd started feeling it that it *wasn't* more than that, but it was. And even worse, it was something *sexual*. Since the moment she'd put on this dress and thought of Max seeing her in it, her entire body had been supercharged with an undeniable sexual tension.

And here she'd thought she was over him. Completely. And totally.

"How do you explain *that*?" she whispered, scowling at herself in the mirror.

Perhaps it had to do with the nature of this case. It centered on sex, after all. And the guy who would want the sex from her was going to be an icky, lecherous thief. But the guy who was supposed to be her husband—her protector, sort of—was *not* icky. Far from it. So that was it. She was being forced to think about sex because of the case and the way it had caused her to dress. And she had to vent those sexual feelings in *some* direction. Which meant Max.

She smiled into the mirror, feeling much better. She still didn't like the way she felt, but maybe it made sense now that she'd given herself a logical explanation. This would go away. It was just a preliminary feeling brought on by the role she was being asked to play.

Hearing footsteps in the hallway, she turned to see Max enter the large foyer where she stood. He gave her a long, slow perusal that turned her hot inside, and in some places more than others. And which also made her think—drat, everything she'd just told herself was obviously a crock.

"Well?" she finally said.

"Sexy as sin itself," he replied, voice seductively low.

She swallowed, hard. Because she could have sworn she'd detected just a trace of emotion this time, a faint hint of passion. Enough to send a wave of heat traveling the length of her spine.

Oh yes, a complete crock of shit, that crap about feeling sexual because it was part of the job. No truth in it whatsoever. She wanted the guy. God help her, but she did. And as for thinking she was over him because she didn't want to sleep next to him—more crap.

Because right now, right at this moment—she *did* want to sleep next to him. Only she didn't want to sleep. She wanted to do other things, and lots of them. It was hitting her hard, nearly stealing her breath. And if she'd been sick before—well, she was sick now, too. Sick with wanting it. Sick over feeling so much for him, even when he obviously detested her. But this time the sickness didn't diminish her desire. Nope, not one little bit.

Nonetheless, she had to pull herself together and try to continue the conversation. "So you think he'll like me then?"

He flashed a knowing look that said *quit playing games*. And then he raked his eyes over her once more, fueling the fire inside her. "Yeah. He'll like you."

Max wore a black Armani suit and looked pretty damn good himself. Okay, more than pretty good. Devastatingly handsome. Which was part of why she was becoming so painfully aware of how much she wanted him. "Aren't you overdressed?" she asked anyway, for the sake of curiosity.

He shook his head. "I just got home from work. I'm a stockbroker, remember."

"Oh, right." And she hadn't meant to imply that she minded at all. Max always looked incredible in an expensive suit. In fact, she couldn't help thinking that they probably made a very striking couple.

It was only a shame that it was all pretend.

With a fresh rush of nervousness, she decided she'd better prepare for whatever was coming because, knowing her "husband," she wouldn't have much of a choice either way. So she took a deep breath and said, "Max, have you thought about...how to convince this guy we're married?"

When he didn't answer right away, she felt silly and went on. "I mean, we don't *act* married."

"We're not *acting* married because the guy's not *here* yet," he said, looking unduly worried. "When he *gets* here, *then* we'll act married." He narrowed his gaze on her critically. "Frank said you could pull this off. You're not going to let me down again, are you?"

The words hit her like a blow to the gut. His veiled, snide comments were one thing, but this was, this was...she was suddenly so furious she could barely think straight. And as for wanting him—well, he'd just very efficiently squelched every ounce of desire that had just been flooding her—which was just as well.

She instantly resolved that she wouldn't sleep with him if he were the last man on earth, and she thought of telling him that, but decided it would be more appropriate to the conversation to say instead, "Of course I can pull it off, you arrogant bastard! And no, I'm not going to let you down. In fact, I'm going to prove to you once and for all exactly how good of a P.I. I am."

"Well, that would be a pleasant surprise."

She glared at him, for lack of any better response—because the only one she could think of was the I-wouldn't-sleep-with-you-if-you-were-last-man-on-earth thing, which might tip him off that she was thinking about sex, and she wasn't about to give him the pleasure of knowing that.

Then she made a concerted effort to calm down, because Carlo Coletti would be here any minute and she couldn't let Max rile her like this—she had to stay professional. She drew in a deep, cleansing breath, tried to banish all the crazy, mixed up emotions from her mind, then spoke in a very calm tone. "I just wanted to know if you'd given any thought to how—"

The chime of the doorbell cut her off. "Show time," he said.

Oh God, what ridiculous timing. She rolled her eyes. And Max placed both his strong hands on her nearly bare shoulders. "Are you ready to be sexy?"

Not particularly. You just ruined that. But she didn't exactly have a choice, did she? And she remained completely determined to show him she could do her job. So she nodded. "Yes. I'm ready."

"Then here we go," he said. And he opened the door.

"Max!" said the man standing on the other side, who was surprisingly youngish and tall and blond, and even kind of handsome. Still, just viewing him from where she stood behind Max, she could sense the smarmy guy lurking beneath the nice sports jacket—something tailored clothes and a handsome face couldn't hide.

"Carlo, come in."

Max stepped back and motioned the other man inside—and then Carlo's eyes fell on her and he stopped cold. Yep, he was sleazy all right. He looked at her in that way—the way other men couldn't see but women could sense, with a stare that bore right through her, demeaning her into a piece of flesh instead of a person.

She couldn't help thinking instantly of Carlo's victims. *You'd have to be in a desperate place to let this guy get the best of you.* But that wasn't her concern right now.

"My God, Max," he said, but he still leered at her—and she smiled her way through it, even forcing herself to meet his gaze. He looked like a guy who'd just hit the jackpot at Caesar's Palace. "*This* is a beautiful woman, Max! Where on earth did you find this delectable creature?"

"Honey, meet Carlo Coletti," Max said with a huge smile.

She held out her hand and Carlo took it, holding onto it too long, until he extended his other hand to squeeze her elbow—always the giveaway of a true letch. Then his voice dropped an octave to say, "It's my deep pleasure to meet such a lovely lady."

"It's very nice to meet you, too, Carlo," she returned, succeeding in sounding incredibly pleasant even as his smarminess seemed to coat her skin. He reeked of it.

That was when Max stepped forward and slid his arm around her, planting his hand firm and warm on her bare shoulder, giving a snug squeeze. "Carlo," he said, "this is my treasure of a wife, Kimberly."

And then he kissed her.

Chapter Five

AND IT WAS no small, chaste kiss, either. He kissed her long and slow and deep, his tongue gliding past her lips, stealing her strength, leaving her instantly weak. Kimberly had no choice but to twine her arms around his neck and hold on lest she faint with the utter deliciousness of him.

Well, this answered one question. Yes, apparently he'd given this some thought.

Actually, it answered *several* questions, the rest of which had to do with her wanting him with every ounce of her being despite him deeming her responsible for lots of bad things in his life. She definitely did. And it was definitely way out of her control.

His tongue touching hers was like electricity, shooting a bolt of lightning straight into the lace panties she wore beneath her sexy dress. His mouth on hers, the very scent of him, the feel of him, all brought back something familiar and masculine and distinctly Max that she remembered and cherished. She clutched at him still, one hand in his hair, bits of it wrapped tenderly in her fist, as her her entire body pulsed with the power of his incredible kiss.

And then he was gone, pulling back, ending it.

And she was trying to breathe again, get her balance, and remembering she had to look sexy and sophisticated in spite of the fact that Max had just kissed her senseless.

"You'll have to forgive me, Carlo," her pretend husband said, tainting his voice with a deep chuckle. "But I was…overcome. When you have a woman like this, you spend every second wanting to be alone with her."

Getting her senses back about her, she couldn't quite believe he'd done it. Because it might have rocked her world, but it didn't seem smart to her, character-wise. He was a stockbroker. They were supposed to be dignified people. She peeked up at Carlo for a reaction.

"Oh, don't apologize," he said. "I understand perfectly." And then he took the opportunity to cast her a wildly lusty look that made her want to retch, but instead she smiled and hoped it reached her eyes.

Which was when she understood—Carlo was as sleazy as sleazy got, and Max had played him correctly. Carlo didn't realize classy people didn't make out while greeting guests at the door. Carlo only wished it could have been him. It had done nothing but fuel his desire for her.

"Shall we have a drink before dinner?" Max suggested, and she flashed *him* a smile, too, because that suddenly seemed to be her business in the last two minutes—kissing and flashing smiles—and he smiled back, a really great smile that pretty much melted everything inside her to molten lava all over again. And then he even put his hand at the small of her back to escort her down the hall.

Though as they walked, and Max and Carlo made manly small talk about Max's Porsche out front, it hit her anew—*Max had kissed her*! Full-on and passionate. The kind of kiss young girls dreamed of. And the kind of kiss older girls wanted more of—and oh, how she wanted more; she'd wanted more the moment his mouth had left hers. It had been the kind of kiss that drenched her soul in desire and heat and weakness and left her knowing the world would never be quite the same again.

She released a long, deep sigh and let the afterglow of it roll through her.

And then she remembered.

Oh God, she'd forgotten so quickly.

It was only pretend.

"To new friends," Carlo said, clinking his glass first against hers, then Max's.

"New friends," Max echoed.

Kimberly only smiled. Like before, it seemed adequate.

But now that she'd recovered—at least somewhat—from Max's unexpected kiss, she decided it was time to get to work. "So, Carlo, Max tells me you want to learn about the stock game." They stood on a vast patio that overlooked the pool, and she took a step closer to him, giving her head what she hoped was a slightly flirtatious tilt.

Carlo smiled, almost sincerely—but he blew it when his gaze dropped ever-so-briefly to her cleavage before lifting it back to her eyes. "It's something I've always wanted to pursue." And now his expression told her that what he was actually interested in pursuing stood right in front of him.

"Then you're not in banking?" she asked, not only to draw out his cover, but also to make him think she was interested in finding out more about him.

Carlo shook his head. "Shipping."

"As in boats?" she asked, confused.

He shook his head again, with a soft laugh. "My company ships merchandise, mostly glassware and fragile items."

"Ah," she said, flicking a short glance to Max. She'd expected their guest to come up with something a little more exotic or at least impressive. "And how did you meet Max?"

"We both frequent Chester's," Max answered for him. She knew the place—an upscale bar on the ground floor of one of the shiny glass office buildings downtown.

"Max is quite a pool shark," Carlo said.

"That he is," she agreed, although she'd never seen Max play pool. But he'd always told her that a good P.I. possessed a variety of skills to help fit into any social setting, and she supposed this was one example—a guy who could play a decent game of pool probably made friends in a bar much easier than a guy who didn't.

"Do *you* play?" Carlo asked, a suggestive light twinkling in his eyes.

She almost released a laugh at what he'd surely intended as a double entendre, but instead held her response to another smile. So far, that seemed to be the only real skill required from her—but when the time came to make their way to the dining room, she steeled herself, knowing things were bound to get more challenging, probably starting now.

MAX LET CARLO take the place at the head of the table, and he and Kimberly took the seats to either side. It was strategic placement—let the guy feel important, let the guy get close to her. At the same time, though, he hoped Carlo wouldn't move in on her too quickly. The idea of the slimeball sliding his hand onto her knee beneath the table rankled.

Max hated the way the guy looked at her. That was why he'd kissed her like that when Carlo had walked in the door—part impulse, part instinct. It was as if he'd thought acting territorial would protect her. And he knew he was *supposed* to want the guy to react to her this way, but maybe it had happened a little easier than he'd expected. Maybe it was going to be a little tougher to play dumb than he had anticipated. He'd thought this role would be a fairly easy one—the real job falling on

Kimberly—but maybe it wouldn't be so easy on his ego to have his "wife" stolen right under his nose while he pretended to be oblivious. Especially by a piece of garbage like Carlo.

Next to him, the thief ogled her. Which was, of course, exactly what he was supposed to do. But already, Max felt the need to interrupt. "So, Carlo, what do you think of the place?" He motioned to their surroundings like a man who was the king of his castle.

"Fabulous, Max. Incredible." But then he turned his gaze right back on Kimberly. "And a wife like this to share it all with? You've got the life, pal. What I wouldn't give to be in your shoes."

Subtle the guy wasn't.

"Oh, now, Carlo," Kimberly said in a half-bashful, half-flattered tone, "you're too kind." Then she fluttered her eyelashes at him like a teenager in heat. Subtlety wasn't her strong suit, either. But, he had to remind himself, her job right now was *not* to be subtle—it was to be *seducible*. By another man. Another rankling idea.

"Where'd you find this beauty, Max, old buddy?"

Old buddy? I'll old buddy you, *asshole*. And what was this guy's fascination about where he and his "wife" had met? But he reined in his irritation and exchanged it for a smile. "We met in college."

Carlo's leer managed to increase and Max imagined thoughts of naughty co-eds dancing through his head. Kimberly was leering right back at him, too, her eyes wide, her lips pretty and pouty with lipstick the color of the red wine they were all drinking. Max's gaze felt stuck to her.

"I knew the moment I saw her," he said without planning it, "that she was the woman for me." And then she turned her hazel eyes on him, which had been his hope. Although he didn't know why. But it made him remember—how some days her eyes seemed more brown, other days gold as amber, and how, at still other times they would glitter green. Tonight they took on a warm honey-colored shade. He didn't hesitate to hold the gaze. "She was wearing a short red skirt and a white blouse, and she had a great tan. It was September."

He watched her tense slightly, then swallow hard, liking the effect the words had had on her. Because that really *was* what she'd been wearing on the day they'd met, although it hadn't been at college. It had been on an elevator—she'd heard him mention being a P.I. and started asking him questions about it.

"We had lunch," she reminded him, her voice silky.

Yes—her questions had turned into an invitation for lunch, and lunch had turned into a job for her. And then more.

"You ordered quiche," he said, their eyes still locked.

He could tell by her expression that this one surprised her—she'd always accused him of having a bad memory for details. She smiled. "That's right."

"What did *I* have?" he quizzed her.

Her expression turned slightly saucy with the game they were playing. "You think I don't remember?"

"Prove me wrong."

"An Italian sub," she smoothly replied. "Extra pepperoni."

He grinned slightly at the correct answer.

"So…" Carlo interrupted uncertainly, drawing Max back to the present, and making it clear he was desperate to be the center of attention again—which Max apparently needed reminding. What had he been doing strolling down memory lane like that, anyway? He couldn't explain it, except to again chalk it up to his ego, something he certainly hadn't expected to come into play here. He'd have to squelch it in the future.

"Sorry about that, Carlo," he said easily. Then glanced down to see that all their glasses were nearly empty. "More wine?"

Though he didn't wait for an answer before excusing himself to get more. He wasn't sure why, but he needed a quick break—from all the sexual tension, he guessed. And to get his head back on straight about what was taking place here. It was only a job, all just a means to an end, catching a crook.

Grabbing the already open bottle from a kitchen counter, he asked Mrs. Leland, the woman he'd hired to cook for them this evening, to uncork another.

Returning to the table with a bottle in each hand, ready to resume the game he'd set in play, he found his guest already ogling his "wife" again—something he'd have no choice but to get used to, and get used to pretending he didn't see, fast.

But maybe this departure from oblivious husband had been good. If the guy truly got a charge out of stealing the wife away from the adoring spouse, Max had set it up perfectly. And it sure hadn't done anything to scare Carlo away.

Feeling completely weirded out, Kimberly looked back and forth between the two men. She had two guys vying for her attention—every woman's fantasy. Except that one of them was a sleazy toad and the other one was pretending. Swell. Okay, so it wasn't a *perfect* fantasy.

"Those are exquisite earrings," Carlo said. Their eyes met—ick, but she worked to maintain the gaze as she leaned a little closer for him to get a better look—and he actually reached over to diddle her earlobe with his fingertip, which made her want to retch. "Lovely necklace, too," he said. And then—wow—his fingers were there, too, touching it, playing with it, and her entire body went rigid. *But smile, damn it. Smile at the jerk.*

"That's just a bauble," Max said across from her as Carlo continued to examine the necklace too closely for her comfort.

She flicked her gaze to Max. Did he look as tense as she felt? Or was she just imagining that?

"She picked it up on our last trip to New York," Max continued with a grin, even if it appeared a little forced. "If you want to see Kimberly's *real* jewelry, you'll have to sweet talk her into showing it to you."

Carlo practically glowed with lust at the suggestion—but he finally pulled his fingers away from her neck, thank goodness. "I'd love to take a look at it sometime."

"Max has been *very* generous," she said, smiling across the table at him—just as Mrs. Leland entered with a tray of dinner salads, which she placed before each of them, one by one.

"Kimberly has a weakness for diamonds, don't you, babe?" Max asked as the cook departed.

And her skin warmed. *Babe.* He used to call her that. Not in the too-forward, casual way, but in the endearing, that's-how-close-we-are way: *What's on TV, babe? What do you want to do tonight, babe? That's a great dress, babe.*

She swallowed. "Yes," she managed. "I have a *horrible* weakness for diamonds." *And a horrible weakness for you.*

But stop it. Stop thinking about Max, and sex, and weaknesses, and get your head back into the game here.

"She wears them constantly," he went on. "Tonight, for instance, a casual dinner with a new friend—out come the diamonds."

Though at this point she thought he might be pouring it on a bit thick, he seemed to know what he was doing where Carlo was concerned, so she decided to follow his lead. "Well, I wanted to look nice for your guest, of course, and make a good impression on him." And she flashed another come-hither smile.

"Oh, you do, and you have," Carlo gushed.

But Max kept right on going. "She actually wears them out shopping sometimes."

"Only to the better stores, honey," she insisted.

"And once, *once*—" Max paused to give another of

those masculine just-between-us-guys laughs, "—I actually found her wearing them as she sat by the pool in her bikini."

"You don't say." It came as no surprise that Carlo looked utterly titillated by the idea.

And so she gave a ridiculous giggle, warming to her part now. "It reeked havoc on my tan lines, but I do enjoy the feel of them next to my skin."

After which Carlo murmured something too low for her to understand—probably some observation about tans or skin. So she blinked, still striving to appear flirtatious and vibrant. "I'm sorry, I missed that. What did you say, Carlo?"

But he got hold of himself. "Oh—I was just saying the pool looked awesome."

She shrugged. "Actually, I find it rather small and keep bugging Max to build me a bigger one." The pool, in fact, was enormous. But she made a pouty face at Max anyway.

"Nothing I love like catching some rays next to a pool," Carlo said.

"Really?" Max replied matter-of-factly. "Well, you'll have to come over for a swim sometime."

"Soon, perhaps," she added in a lilting voice.

Then Carlo tilted his head and glanced coyly back and forth between them. "You know…" he began, but then he stopped and shook his head. "Wait. Never mind."

"What is it?" she prodded.

Carlo lowered his chin sheepishly. "Oh, it's nothing."

"No, really, what were you going to say?"

"Well," he paused and shook his head almost helplessly, "I was just thinking—my place is being painted this weekend..."

"Actually, I've never heard you say where you live, Carlo," Max commented, more from curiosity about how he would reply, she suspected, than anything else.

"Oh, I've got a huge condo near the beach. In Malibu. It's...just been remodeled. That's why it's being painted." Hmm, not exactly the dumpy side of Venice.

"Sounds lovely," she said. "But what does that have to do with...whatever we were talking about?" She giggled at her own forgetfulness, figuring that playing dumb, or a little drunk, might add to her assets in his eyes.

Again, Carlo looked hesitant. "Well, I was just thinking it would be a perfect time to chill at your pool, but...I wouldn't want to impose, so just forget I said anything." He shook his head.

"Why should we forget it?" she replied quickly. "I think it's a wonderful idea. Max and I have no plans at all this weekend, do we, honey?"

"None at all." Max gave his head a short shake now, too.

"But there's no need for you to sleep in those nasty fumes," she went on. "Why don't you just stay here tonight and tomorrow we can all enjoy the pool together.

I'm sure Max has as spare pair of trunks."

Carlo feigned shock at such a generous offer. "Are you sure? It wouldn't be an imposition?" Which struck her as quite silly, since he'd practically invited himself.

But it was easier to just play along. "Tomorrow's Saturday," she replied. "And we have plenty of guestrooms. So why not? You don't mind, do you, Max?"

She shifted her gaze back to him. And he smiled. The discussion about the pool had played right into their plans. "Of course not. We'd love to have you."

And I'd *love to have* you. The words flitted through her mind as it was yanked mercilessly from her work just by looking into Max's dark eyes.

"Well, thanks. That's great," Carlo was saying––but she barely even heard him. Instead, she suddenly found herself turning her come-hither smile on *Max*—glad she could do it under the guise of her role, but inside still wishing that it wasn't all just pretend.

Chapter Six

AFTER TAKING AWAY the salad bowls, Mrs. Leland served salmon, twice-baked potatoes, and fresh bread. Kimberly listened as Max took the opportunity to talk stocks and bonds with Carlo—another impressive skill he'd apparently picked up somewhere along the way—and she bowed out of the conversation other than to add an occasional comment to help keep Carlo focused on *her*.

As the charade went on, she found herself wading through the mire of wanting Max more and more with each passing minute. Even when she worked to bait Carlo with her flirtations, she stayed painfully aware of Max's presence, and couldn't keep her thoughts from straying to past times—better times—shared with him.

"Kimberly?"

She jolted to attention. "Huh?" She looked up to see Max and Carlo both rising from their chairs.

"I said," Max told her very calmly, "let's retire to the living room for a while." And he raised his eyebrows at her as if to say *pay attention,* and she thought, *swell, great way to show him what a skilled P.I. I am.*

But all her bad feelings were quelled when she took a seat on the big sofa in front of the massive stone fireplace and Max sat down next to her, close, sliding his arm warmly around her shoulder. Her heart fluttered. Along with a few other choice body parts, as well. This husband-and-wife thing definitely had its benefits, even if it *was* only make-believe.

Carlo settled in a roomy easy chair nearby and, over the next few minutes, started looking a little antsy, but Max acted as if he didn't notice and proceeded to talk some more about his imaginary career in investments.

"Which reminds me," he finally said, "I've got a business call to make—need to touch base with a colleague in Japan. Will you excuse me for a few minutes?"

And then he was gone, quick as that, up off the couch and out of the room. Disappointment ran rampant through Kimberly's limbs.

And a business call? At ten o'clock on a Friday night? Well, Max had cleverly thrown in the Japan thing—she supposed it was daytime there right now. Daytime on Saturday, now that she thought about it, but maybe he was counting on Carlo not know that. Regardless, she knew this meant it was time to get down to some more of *her* business, time to start flirting with Carlo *in private* and letting him begin to think she might be interested in fooling around.

It took him about half a second to make the first move. He rose from his chair and joined her on the couch. Too close for her liking, but part of the job. And she'd done this kind of work on occasion before, so she knew how to handle it. But most guys, even bad guys, weren't as outright lecherous as this one. And she'd never before done this sort of job when her mind and body were so desperately tied up in wanting another man.

"Hi," he said. His eyes practically twinkled with the new seclusion they shared.

She made herself smile back at him, look a bit coquettish. "Hi."

And then he reached out and fingered the thin shoulder strap of her dress. "You're a beautiful woman, Kimberly."

This guy really needs to work on his originality. But she forged ahead. "Why, Carlo, you're going to make Max jealous with all these compliments."

"They're all true," he said. "But Max doesn't matter."

Wow, he was quick. She put on her best innocent face. "Max doesn't matter?"

"I just mean…he's not here right now. It's just me and you."

She nodded, for lack of any better move.

Carlo withdrew his fingers from beneath the strap of her dress and once again slid them to the thin diamond necklace she wore. "I'm still quite taken by this, Kimberly."

"Thank you, Carlo."

"Is all your jewelry truly this exquisite?"

Okay, he was more than quick—he was a regular

speed demon. But she took the opening. "As I said at dinner, this is really just a smallish piece. My collection upstairs consists of much more elaborate jewels."

He nodded, looking utterly attentive. "So you keep them on the premises. Is that safe?"

Like earlier, she wanted to laugh. And she began to wonder for the first time just how stupid these victimized couples had been. But she could only guess that maybe they hadn't come across as being as totally inviting as she and Max had, which was possibly making Carlo comfortable being this forward. Or perhaps the wives had truly been attracted to him. She saw straight through him for the slime he was, but if you didn't...well, he was nice enough to look at and she could imagine him—the things he said and way he touched so freely—being intimidatingly persuasive. And some women were more impressionable than her.

"They're in a safe in our bedroom so I *hope* they're secure enough," she said after a brief hesitation. "And if I kept them in some silly safe deposit box somewhere, it would be much harder to wear them, wouldn't it?"

She giggled and the schmuck joined in her laughter, gently lowering a hand to her knee. Inside, she tensed at the touch, but didn't let it show. "Say," he began, "maybe while we're waiting for Max to finish with his call, you could let me see some of your prized gems. Hearing you talk about them has intrigued me."

Nope, too soon. She and Max hadn't even begun to synchronize the theft yet, and anything could happen.

Yes, Max had suggested Carlo ask to see the jewelry, but that had been bait for later. "Oh, we've got plenty of time for that, now that you're staying," she told him. And when she sensed him getting ready to lean closer, she rose to her feet. "How about some brandy?"

"All right, sure."

Though as she hurried to the bar across the room, he stood up and followed her. Geez, he was easily the most aggressive man she'd ever met.

Having familiarized herself with the liquor cabinet, she pulled out a decanter half-filled with brandy, along with two snifters. She poured one and handed it to him before pouring another for herself. After recapping the decanter, she picked up her snifter and turned—to find Carlo standing, as usual, far too close for comfort.

"Let's toast," he said, lifting a hand to her arm. His thumb began to stroke her skin. "To diamonds. And to you. Two of the world's natural beauties."

MAX LEANED BACK in the executive leather chair in the study. Propping his feet on the desk, he glanced around. Built-in ebony bookcases, housing old volumes with rich leather spines he could smell, surrounded him. To his left, a huge picture window looked out on the front lawn. To his right, a framed map of the world hung on the wall. He studied the map stuck with pins that seemed to indicate destinations visited. *But if you had all this why would you need to look any further?*

Carlo's words came back to him. *And a wife like this to share it all with? You've got the life, pal.* The thief had been right about that—a place like this, a wife like Kimberly ...

But wait a minute.

The last thing Max needed was a wife like Kimberly. Sure, he didn't like seeing Carlo all over her, but that didn't mean he was ready to marry her. Or even engage in any relationship at all. There was one thing he didn't have with Kimberly that happened to be a major relationship essential: trust.

He'd left her alone with Carlo strictly to give the guy the opportunity to start making his move, start trying to lure her away from Max while he wasn't around to fawn over her. He kind of hated doing that, but he knew she could handle it. She'd been a quick study at the P.I. thing until lousing up the Carpenter case. And that wasn't a skills problem—it was ethics.

Skills she had. Which was good, because she'd need them with this creep. And Frank wouldn't have sent her if he'd had any doubts she could do it. And even *he* had to admit she'd become a good actress. Maybe a little *too* good. She'd been fine with undercover gigs before, but he'd never cast her as anything like this—a sexy, *ready* kind of woman. And she was pulling it off without a hitch. It irritated him to know Carlo thought she really liked him.

Frankly, Carlo was worse than he'd expected. He kind of wanted to kill the jerk, thinking about how excited the guy had gotten watching him kiss her, hoping to steal her away at the same time. Oh well, at least they hadn't wasted any time making sure Carlo viewed her in a sexual light. Not that Max liked him thinking of her that way. He didn't.

And just why the hell was that again? His ego. Just his ego.

"Mr. Tate?"

Looking up to see Mrs. Leland in the office doorway, he welcomed the distraction—he was starting to obsess over this situation and he didn't like it. "Yes, Mrs. Leland?"

"I've finished cleaning up dinner, so I'll be going now."

"All right. Thank you for letting me know."

She smiled. "Everything was to your liking?"

"Everything was great."

"And your case. It goes well?"

"So far, so good," he told her. Then he lowered his feet to the floor and stood up. "I'll walk you out."

He'd used the older woman for such events before and had come to like her. She whipped up a spectacular meal and he could see that, however timidly, she found it exciting to do work for a private investigator.

"Would you like me to tell the young lady goodnight, and the other gentleman? I could thank her for giving me the weekend off while he's standing there listening."

Max smiled—he'd told Mrs. Leland to pretend she

worked there full-time if it came up around Carlo when serving dinner. "That won't be necessary," he replied. "I mentioned it to him in passing already. But thanks for thinking of it."

When they reached the door, he pulled out his wallet and pushed a fifty dollar bill into her hand. She raised her gaze to him, clearly astonished. "What's this for? I'll be sending my regular invoice to your office."

He gave her a small grin. "A tip. For services well-rendered." When her eyes lit up, he added, "Put this toward Joey's college expenses." With three kids, the oldest a freshman at Cal State, he suspected jobs like this one were important to her family.

"Well, thank you, Mr. Tate," she said, still smiling.

He opened the massive front door to let her out. "Have a safe drive home, Mrs. Leland."

He stood just beyond the threshold, watching as she got in her car and drove away. Then he looked up at the sky—or more precisely, the stars. You could see them here in the hills in much more abundance than from his place closer to the city. Too many *lights* in the city. Out here, it was easy to forget the city even existed. Warm night air surrounded him. *Yep, a guy could get used to this.*

Oh, he'd never have the bucks for a place *this* ornate. But a man didn't need such extreme luxuries to be happy. Once he'd thought he did. Doing well in Vegas had started to make him a little greedy, hence his Porsche. But since he'd made the decision to get out of the field and just run the company, he'd done some practical thinking about what it took to be fulfilled.

There was no sin in owning some nice things, but he'd started figuring out that he was happiest just being a middle-of-the-road kind of guy. A beer and pretzels guy who drove a Porsche. A corner bar guy who wore Armani suits to work. He was achieving a happy medium. Finding the right balance of everything he needed to feel good when he got up in the morning and went to bed at night. And life was looking pretty fine at the moment. *And a wife like this to share it all with? You've got the life, pal.*

What the hell? Where had that thought come from?

But Max had no time to contemplate the answer. Because that was when Kimberly screamed.

Chapter Seven

MAX BOLTED TOWARD the living room, ready to tear Carlo Coletti limb from sleazy limb.

But he burst in only to find Carlo holding the stem of a broken glass, his shirt and jacket stained with dark liquid, and Kimberly saying, "Oh, I'm so sorry, Carlo!"

"What the hell happened?" Max asked.

They both looked up. "I'm so embarrassed," she said. "Carlo made a toast and I'm afraid I clinked our snifters too hard. I broke them both and got brandy all over him."

Max's body flooded with relief, even though his heart still pounded against his ribs. Everything was okay here. Carlo wasn't attacking her. She wasn't hurt. Nothing was wrong.

"We'll have your clothes dry cleaned, of course," she was telling Carlo as she bent to grab some small towels from a cabinet beneath the bar, making Max grateful she'd checked out the place so well and knew just where such things were kept.

She blotted one awkwardly against Carlo's chest,

making Max cringe inside. Little snake—even now, he was drawing her touch. Sort of, anyway. Thank God it was only sort of, or he'd be going crazy.

And then he flinched. What was happening inside him? Why this crazed reaction to Kimberly doing her job?

Ego, ego, ego.

Just keep telling yourself that, buddy.

"Oh no," Carlo said then, his eyes planted squarely on Kimberly's breasts. "Looks like the brandy splashed on you, too."

Shifting his gaze, Max saw that indeed her chest was soaking wet. And Carlo was reaching for one of the dry towels.

Max's spine went ramrod straight. *No way in hell.* He rushed forward and snatched the towel from Carlo's fist. "Babe," he said, "you really must be more careful." And then he tenderly pressed the towel against the low neckline of her dress, gently blotting away the wetness.

He tensed when he she pulled in her breath, and their gazes met. He hadn't meant to startle her. He'd only wanted to protect her from Carlo. *Sorry.* He mouthed the word, his back to the slimy rat.

"It's all right." Her reply came in a breathy whisper.

And their gazes stayed locked. And he thought he glimpsed longing in her eyes. Thought he felt her *wanting* him to touch her there—but without the towel.

And he hoped like hell he was wrong. Because this was no time for that. *No time* was the time for that. Not with them—not anymore.

Yet her breasts were lush beneath his touch, the thin towel the only barrier between her flesh and his hands. And the hell of it was that it would be easy to want her, so damn easy…

"Max," she said, loud enough that it shook him alert, "you'll need to get Carlo something else to wear."

"You're right," he replied, finally pulling the towel away from her damp skin and tossing it aside. "Why don't you change, too, babe? I'll come with you and find something for Carlo."

"Sure," she said, then turned to the other man—who once again had been ousted from a clandestine moment between them and didn't look happy about it. "Relax and help yourself to something else in the liquor cabinet, Carlo. We'll be back in just a few."

As they exited the room, Max pressed his palm to the small of her back where her little black dress hugged her curves. But as they climbed the stairs, his thoughts were drawn back to the sound of her scream, and to the way it had run through him like a sword.

An overreaction on her part, big time. Not an I-broke-a-glass-and-made-a-mess kind of scream. An I'm-being-molested kind of scream.

And for the first time since it had happened, he had the chance to start getting angry. At the top of the stairs, he grabbed her wrist and spun her to face him. "Don't ever do that again," he snapped, though he kept his tone low enough that Carlo wouldn't hear.

Her eyes looked darker now, more brown, in the dim lighting of the upstairs hall. "Do what?"

"Don't scream like that unless you mean it."

"I meant it."

But he kept right on going, his ire reaching a fever pitch now. "Do you know how badly that scared me? Do you know what I thought was happening to you in there? You don't scream like that unless something's really wrong, Brandt. Got it?"

Got it, she was supposed to reply. But she didn't.

Instead, her voice came out hushed and snide. "Something *was* wrong. And breaking those glasses wasn't an accident. The guy's hand was lingering dangerously close to my breasts, and he was ready to pounce. I had the feeling I might not be able to hold him off. So I went with my impulse and slammed my glass into his.

"And for your information, I kind of felt like I needed you in there. You abandoned me without warning. I know this is my job, but *your* job is to be there if I need you, remember? So I'll scream whenever I damn well feel like screaming. Now, do *you* got it?"

Max blinked. Damn, he'd had no idea Carlo would make a move like that so fast, one heavy enough to put her in panic mode. And she was right—he should've been there. He'd misjudged Carlo's technique. And he'd also been selfish—not wanting to have to watch the jerk get close to her.

He took a deep breath. "You're right. I'm sorry, Brandt. I should've been keeping an eye on things."

"And just so you know, I need a break. So I'm not going back down there."

"That's fine," he said. "I'll handle it."

She was still glaring at him like she wanted to flay him alive, though—until finally she turned and stalked toward the master suite. He started to follow, when suddenly she stopped and whirled to face him again, one finger in the air. "But this doesn't mean I can't handle the guy, Tate."

"I didn't say it did."

"Because I can. I can do my job, and you'd better not start thinking I can't."

"Brandt, I didn't—"

"I'm not the same woman you knew, Tate. I'm no shrinking violet. I'm a lot tougher than before, a lot more capable. Got it?"

What could he say to all that? Judging by what he'd seen so far, it seemed a completely valid self-assessment. "Got it."

KIMBERLY STEPPED FROM the oversize shower, glad to feel clean. Clean of the brandy. Clean of Carlo's disgusting touches.

Beyond the bathroom door, she heard movement in the master suite. "Tate, is that you?"

"Yeah, it's me."

Stepping into the enormous closet, conveniently attached to the bathroom, she looked through her own contributions to the clothing that hung there. She pulled one of the nighties she'd brought from a satin-covered hanger, more than a little nervous about putting it on, but worry was useless at this point. Of course, had she known the kind of reaction she'd end up having to Max, she'd have definitely brought a wider variety of sleepwear. As it was, she was stuck wearing the short, pink, lacy nightgown that was really more of a slip.

She changed into it with her back to the mirror, not wanting to see how much it revealed. And whether or not worry was useless, it was also seemingly impossible to prevent—even without looking in the mirror, she knew this thing was practically see-through.

What on earth had she been thinking when she packed? *Bring sexy clothes,* Max had told her. *That* was what she'd been thinking. So she'd ravaged her closets and drawers for items that seemed sexy with little time to measure practicality. And now she had to walk out into the bedroom—the bedroom they had to *share*—and face him in *this.*

But they were claiming to be professionals here, right? *So…just act normal. Act normal—and so will Max.* It was that simple.

"Is Carlo all settled in for the night?" she asked through the door. A good, sensible, normal kind of question.

"I showed him to one of the guestrooms, gave him some sweats to wear, and he went back down to watch TV," Max replied on the other side. "He seemed disappointed, of course, that you didn't come back down with me."

"Yeah, well, I've had about as much Carlo Coletti as I can stand for one night." After the brandy incident, she'd been more than ready to call it a day. And Max couldn't say she hadn't earned her pay tonight.

"Mind if I ask you a question, out of curiosity?" Max asked then.

"Sure." She returned to the bathroom and ran a brush through her hair, having kept it dry in the shower.

"After seeing the way Carlo behaves around you," Max said, "I find myself wondering—why would all these well-to-do women sleep with this raunchy guy? Frankly, I'm baffled. Can you shed any light on that?"

Still brushing her hair, she gave a light shrug even though he couldn't see her. "He's sort of a handsome man, Tate."

"He is?"

She smiled to herself, amused at how shocked he sounded. "Well, yeah. Sure, he's a jerk and an obvious letch, but if a woman were, say, suffering from low self-esteem or in a bad marriage or something, maybe she would choose not to see that. Maybe having a guy fall all over you and give you compliments could make you feel special or something."

It took Max a minute to reply. "What about *you*? He didn't make *you* feel special or something, did he?"

He almost sounded jealous. *Almost.* But she decided his question more likely stemmed from fear that she'd soften toward Carlo and botch things up—that he was afraid this was just another version of the Carpenter case all over again.

Still, she kept her cool and answered without getting upset. "No, he makes *me* feel creeped-out. But I'm just not sure all women would realize what kind of a guy he is. I know it seems obvious to you. And to me, too. But women thrive on flattery, Tate. And if a woman feels alone or neglected or something, well, I could see it happening."

"Hmm." That was all he said. So she didn't know what he thought of her response, if he was out there doubting her abilities again or something.

Though at the moment, she had other things to worry about. Because she was done getting ready for bed, but she was still standing in front of the mirror and…yikes—this nightie *was* revealing!

Act normal. Just act normal. She took a deep, fortifying breath.

I'm coming out now. She thought about announcing that through the door. But that wouldn't exactly be very normal, would it? So she held her tongue and prepared to exit, her stomach battling more of those grenade-wielding butterflies that she'd become acquainted with since seeing Max again. Oh boy, this wasn't gonna be easy. *Think normal*, she commanded herself.

She took a deep breath and twisted the doorknob. Then pulled the door open and casually entered the bedroom. Max lay on the bed wearing a pair of white drawstring pajama pants, no shirt. He looked *so* good. Which didn't help her nervousness one bit.

Walking around to the other side of the bed, she remained thankfully unnoticed—until he glanced up from the magazine he was flipping through.

"Is that what you brought to sleep in?" She could feel his eyes on her, practically aghast.

Swallowing hard, she forced herself to look at him. "Well," she explained, "I didn't think ratty pajamas would really fit my new image."

"He's won't be *in bed* with us, Brandt."

She pulled back the covers. "Well, you said it was possible he'd sneak around in the night or something weird like that. I thought he might see me."

"Too much of you."

His eyes stayed glued to her.

And his tone almost made her think...no, couldn't be.

But then, there *had* been that kiss. That soul-stirring, weaken-your-knees kiss. He'd even used his tongue.

"I thought letting him see too much of me was the idea here," she pointed out. And she knew she shouldn't say the rest of what was in her head, knew it was a stupid, crazy thought—but she was tired, and when she got tired she sometimes couldn't think clearly enough to stop herself from saying stupid, crazy things. "You sound jealous, Tate."

He slanted her a look that said, *You've got to be kidding*. "Don't be ludicrous. And the idea is to be *friendly* to the guy, Brandt—not incite him to attack you."

She chose not to reply. But as she slid beneath the sheets—made of some kind of fabulous silk that felt glorious next to her skin—she wondered if that was what *Max* wanted to do, attack her. He said no, of course. But his eyes said yes.

Though that was when she remembered. She'd never been able to *read* his eyes. What looked like lust to her was just as likely annoyance, or maybe even some kind of disgust. And besides, when would she get it through her thick head, once and for all? Everything Max did in front of Carlo was pretend. And everything he did *away* from Carlo was belligerent. Even if he *had* tolerated her outrage in the hall. But she'd been justified about that and he knew it. Any way you sliced it, this was still all business.

She only wished it were that way for *her*—all business. She wished she saw Max as only a co-worker. Because how on earth was she was going to sleep next to him like this—on silk sheets, no less—without going crazy? She shook her head in frustration against the fluffy silk-covered pillow beneath her, then pulled the covers up over her breasts, pressing her bare arms to her sides above the sheets. *Think normal, think normal, think normal.*

Oh, who was she kidding? This was about as far from normal as any situation she'd ever been in. And what she felt for Max—in every sensuously-charged fiber of her body at the moment—was far from normal, too. She had a feeling it was going to be a very long night.

"Ready for lights out?" he asked.

"Sure." Only then she turned to look at him. "Though…when you say lights out, you mean, like, for a little while. Until you get your imaginary call, right?"

Max turned the question over in his head, then told her what he'd been thinking. "I've decided we'll hold off on that."

And she blinked, looking understandably surprised. "What are you talking about?"

"You've had a long night with Carlo."

"But I took the break I needed and—"

"And you've had a long night, like I said," he told her again, the words coming out a little sterner than he intended. "Since he's staying over and we have the whole weekend, we'll postpone the theft until tomorrow."

"When?" She sounded put out, like she thought he was blaming her for something.

"I don't know yet. When the time is right."

"The time seems right enough to me right now," she told him. "I don't see any reason to stretch this out."

He could see her point, could see why she just wanted to be done with it.

But the timing didn't feel right to *him*, even if he couldn't put his finger on why. Maybe because they'd all had a few drinks and he wasn't sure he or Kimberly were at their sharpest. Maybe he'd decided the theft couldn't happen with her wearing that tiny little bit of clingy fabric she had on, that it left her too vulnerable to unwanted groping from their "guest." But whatever the reason, what it came down to was, "Well, I'm the boss and I make the calls, and this is the call I'm making. Now—ready for lights out?"

She replied with a disgruntled sigh and an exaggerated roll of her eyes. "Whatever you say, Tate."

Good enough. Especially since that was likely as good as it was going to get. So he set his magazine aside, reached up and flipped the switch that darkened the room, then settled on his back with one thought in his head. *What a relief.*

But then again, not really. The only real relief was that the room was dark and he could quit trying to look so unaffected by the sight of her. Yet affected he was.

He'd seen her nipples through that silky pink fabric. A dark, rosy color, they'd been poking prominently against the front of her sexy little gown. What had she been thinking—bringing *that* to wear to bed with him? Not to mention to seduce Carlo in—a notion that nearly made him shudder with revulsion.

Well, the answer didn't matter. What mattered was that the picture of those taut, rose-colored buds had planted itself firmly in his mind now and he knew there was no way he'd quit thinking about her any time soon.

He wanted desperately to roll over and touch her breasts. He wanted to kiss their enticing peaks. He remembered Kimberly's breasts clearly—*too* clearly. Round and soft and very sensitive, they'd filled his hands perfectly. Her nipples had always beaded instantly when he touched them, and they'd hardened into tiny pebbles against his tongue.

And God, it would be easy, *so* easy...but no longer just easy to want her—the fact was, he already did. He didn't want to feel that way—he wanted to keep right on denying it—but he was hard as a rock beneath the covers and there was no denying *that*.

Now it would be easy to roll over onto her. To plant another of those full, deep kisses on her perfect mouth. To take those two sweet mounds of flesh into his eager hands. To press his aching erection into the place where he knew she was soft and warm.

Get hold of yourself, Tate. You're on the job here, for God's sake—quit acting like a fourteen-year-old boy who just saw his first naked woman.

He rolled over away from her to be sure he didn't make a tent of the covers. And he decided that she'd been right earlier—this *was* inappropriate, them sleeping next to each other. But he hadn't planned on feeling this way, hadn't really expected it at all, so he hadn't foreseen this problem.

And, well, she was pissed at him now anyway for changing the plan—among other things probably—and that was actually good, under the circumstances. One more reason to push down his lust.

But damn it, on top of everything else, she smelled good, too. Like the after-bath spray he remembered she loved—a sexy, musky scent that always made him think of summertime heat. She must still put it on each night before she went to bed. How would he last the night—smelling her like this, remembering the sight of her breasts through that sheer little gown, wanting to feel her and taste her?

He rolled onto his back again. And then he rolled once more, to face her, to watch her sleeping in the faint glow of the moonlight that shone dimly through the windows.

She was beautiful. More now than before. Earlier, in that dress made for sin, she'd looked beyond hot, beyond steamy. But now, like this—she was just a plain natural beauty, simple with her bed-tousled hair and lips half-parted in sleep, the lipstick gone to leave them a familiar color, like slightly faded berries.

Either way, it didn't matter—the lust he felt for either side of her was equal. And intense.

And he knew that if he stayed in this bed much longer, he'd be reaching out his hand beneath the sheets and…

Come on, Tate, shake this off now. You're a professional—act like it.

Finally, he pushed back the covers and got out of bed. He couldn't sleep here and not have her. Taking his pillow, he made his way to one of the chairs across the room by the fireplace, where he'd just have to suffer until morning.

KIMBERLY AWOKE TO the songs of birds beyond the

balcony door and to the surprise of waking itself—she'd not expected to ever fall asleep last night.

Getting in bed with him for what she'd thought of as *fake* sleep had been challenging enough, especially given her reckless choice of sleepwear. But to then find out she was expected to spend the entire night in bed with him—oh, the sweet, horrid torture of it! She'd pretended to fall asleep immediately, but her skin had prickled with want, and it had been all she could do not to reach out and touch him.

Now she rolled slowly in Max's direction, cautiously easing her eyes open.

But he was gone!

She sat up in bed, startled. Yet just as quickly she spotted him—across the room, curled impossibly in a chair by the fireplace, one leg stretched across the marble table next to it.

Her heart sank a little at the sight. Sleeping next to him had been difficult, but that didn't mean she'd wanted him to leave. Just being close to him—whether or not they touched—made her feel so…alive.

She slumped back against her pillow. *Well, so much for feeling alive.* She hadn't imagined being next to her would be so offensive to him that he'd actually get up and go away. He must harbor even more resentment for her than she understood. And maybe even more than *he* understood. After all, it had been *his* plan that they share the room, and the bed.

She rolled back over the other way, facing away from

him, and shut her eyes tight, holding back tears. A P.I. didn't cry. Especially not one who was determined to show her old boss she was worthy of her job. *Be tough, Kimberly.*

She'd had no trouble being tougher, surer, cockier, these past three years since parting ways with him. Because she'd *had* to be. She'd had to let her personality take on new dimensions in order to keep her emotions out of her work.

But Max...well, he was enough to bring all those old feelings—all of those old pieces of her—rushing back. And she didn't know what she could possibly do to stop it. Part of her regretted ever taking this job on for Frank. And part of her dreaded it ending and never seeing Max again. But the only thing that mattered now was getting her game face back on and finding out what this next day held in store for "Mrs. Max Tate."

Chapter Eight

THREE HOURS LATER, Kimberly lay stretched out next to the fabulous pool in her bikini, in an equally fabulous lounge chair. Next to her, the water sparkled beneath the sun in aqua splendor. Potted palms dotted the area, vibrant summer flowers in bright yellows and hot pinks lining the perimeter. White lawn furniture sat scattered about, the tables covered with enormous turquoise umbrellas, and hidden speakers sent music wafting over the scene to make it complete. She lay back and sighed with the grandeur of it all—L.A. wasn't the Caribbean, but today it came close.

Another heavenly aspect of the moment? She was blessedly alone in her sunny paradise, at least for now. Carlo and Max had gone out to get steaks for the grill. And she desperately needed this private time. She had to regroup—from everything that had already happened. And she had to prepare—for everything yet to take place.

For one thing, she'd grown suddenly squeamish about having Carlo's eyes on her in a bikini. Normally, she didn't have qualms about hiding her body, but it was different when a man looked at you like *that*. Given the lecherous quality she'd instantly sensed in him, she found herself hoping Max would be around for the duration of their sunning and swimming.

Then again, she was practically just as squeamish about being around Max right now, too—only in a different way. She felt embarrassed that he'd left the bed. And she'd even wondered if he'd somehow been able to feel her wanting him so badly, if somehow the vibes had slinked across the silk sheets and onto him.

They hadn't discussed it this morning. She'd fallen back asleep and by the time she reawakened, he had showered and dressed. And he'd conveniently stepped out onto the balcony while she scurried from the bed to the bathroom, all the more aware of what she still wore.

Releasing a long sigh into the balmy air, she remembered promising herself she wouldn't give in to her desires for him—yet that kiss before dinner had quickly done her in and now she felt helpless.

But wait. Stop. Helpless was a terrible word and something she never wanted to be, let alone because a *man* made her feel that way. So as she'd told herself this morning, this would be a good time to refocus on her original goals for this job. She needed to show Max she wouldn't let him down. Which meant being tough. And she needed to survive being near him without going crazy with lust or letting it impede her job performance in any way.

A tall order. But she could do it. She *would* do it.

Only she would do it later. Right now—this was *her* time. To bask in the sun, and the luxury of it all. To clear her mind and get re-energized. To let the rays soak all the tension away. She closed her eyes as the soft sounds of the music filled her, as the warmth of the sun lulled her into relaxation.

MAX WAS GLAD he'd noticed a supermarket nearby as he and Kimberly had driven to the mansion yesterday, or he wouldn't have known where to go for steaks. Carlo wasn't the sharpest knife in the cutting block, but even *he* might have found it suspicious if Max didn't know where they bought groceries.

Now they meandered the aisles together, Max covering his lack of store knowledge by explaining that Mrs. Leland did most of their shopping, and that anything else they needed, Kimberly usually picked up.

"Gorgeous woman, Kimberly," Carlo said.

Max just wanted to shake his head at the guy. How many times had Carlo made the same comment since he'd met her? *Get a new line, pal. And remember you're talking to her husband.* But Carlo seemed so completely taken by her that if he had any sense at all, it had obviously vanished.

"Yes, she certainly is," Max said, his stock reply. And then he spotted the meat counter in the back of the sprawling store. "This way."

"Bet she's something in bed," Carlo snickered under

his breath.

Okay, was this guy serious? He wasn't even sure if Carlo had intended him to hear that, but either way—what a total clod! Under any other circumstances, Max would have punched the imbecile in the mouth.

But punching Carlo in the mouth wasn't on the agenda here. *Stay cool. Play dumb. That's your role, annoying as it is.* So he gave a throaty, knowing laugh and said, "I don't divulge trade secrets."

And then he remembered that if he *did* divulge trade secrets…he'd have said that she was *outstanding* in bed, that making love to Kimberly was, in fact, a sublime experience. Not that he could speak from *recent* experience, but those kinds of memories didn't fade.

Max ordered the steaks from the butcher while Carlo went off in search of beer. And while he waited for the meat to be wrapped, he found his mind drifting back to what had happened last night, or more precisely, to what had *not* happened. Apparently, Kimberly didn't even have to be *doing* anything in bed to drive him wild—just sleeping near her was enough to set him on fire. He shook his head at the insanity of it.

Only now was it occurring to him that he'd been so in heat over her that he'd lain there obsessing over it, not even thinking about Carlo, or the case, or the fact that they were under the same roof as him. Carlo had been lying in the next room still planning to rob them—he knew that much. So, in effect, the thief had been on the job and he hadn't. Hs partner had completely taken over his mind. *Not exactly good form, Tate.*

Well, it was just a damn good thing he'd gotten out of bed. And one thing was for sure—this had been a wake up call. He couldn't let her keep distracting him. The job depended on it. And his client was depending on it, too. So that was it. From now on, he'd shape up and take control of this thing. No more juvenile reactions. No more thinking with his pants.

As Carlo returned, a six-pack of beer tucked under each arm, Max put on his game face. *Now back to work.* And that meant doing exactly what would reel old Carlo in, turning things back toward his "wife" and dropping a line that would come in handy later, when they put the sting in motion.

"Kimberly will really enjoy grilling out this afternoon," he said. "We have that huge area for entertaining, but with just the two of us, and me being so busy at work, we don't make much use of it."

"Spend a lot of time at work, do you?"

Max held back his smile. Carlo had taken his bait perfectly. "Yeah. I'm stuck there late a lot. Sometimes I even get called in on weekends. I know Kimberly gets tired of spending so much time on her own."

"Weekends, too, huh? That's rough. Happen often?"

Max pretended to concentrate on the vast array of snack chips he'd turned to study while waiting for their steaks. "Um, yeah, pretty regularly."

Carlo's eyes widened earnestly. "Well, I hope you don't get called in this afternoon—I'm looking forward to these steaks," he said with a smile. "But if you do…"

"Yeah?" Max scooped up a bag of tortilla chips.

"Well, at least Kimberly won't be left alone. I'll be there to keep her company."

Max grinned and even patted Carlo on the back. "I guess that's true. And I can tell she's enjoying getting to know you."

"Oh?"

Max played it off as nothing. "Well, it's quiet in that big house, even when I *am* home. I just get the idea sometimes…well, that she might like a change of pace, you know?"

Carlo let his smile deepen, clearly reading into the words exactly what Max wanted him to.

Although that imaginary call into the office might not come until tomorrow now, Max had decided. It wasn't that he wanted to keep stretching this thing out—it already seemed interminably long—but he didn't want to be obvious by rushing it. Carlo had spent four days with Max's client before he'd made the move to seduce her and steal her jewelry. And now that the game was afoot, he got the distinct impression Carlo liked the lead-up, liked mooching off them, liked thinking he was building a rapport with Max at the same time he was building a flirtation with Kimberly.

Of course, maybe his client's husband hadn't been as blind and encouraging as Max—maybe it had just taken that long for seduction to come into play. But the more Max studied this piece of sludge, the more one day just seemed too soon. Two would be better. Let him mooch a little more. Let him see Max's blindness a little longer. Let him get revved up for Max's "wife" a little more completely. Let him get sucked in by the lure of his own scheme.

"That reminds me," Max added. "Kimberly wondered if you'd like to stay the whole weekend—let those paint fumes settle a while? What do you say?"

That smile of Carlo's now stretched from ear to ear. "Sounds great!"

Thought it would, Max wanted to mumble. But he held it in.

Upon returning to the house, he immediately suggested that Carlo go back to his place and pick up enough clothes for a couple days. "I'll heat up the grill while you're gone," he said, waving as the other man departed. And then he turned away, glad to let the smile fade, glad to quit acting for a few minutes. That was why he'd insisted Carlo go to the store with him—besides not wanting to leave Kimberly alone with the guy, he wanted to make sure she had an ample break before resuming her role. Now he'd discovered *he* needed one, too. It would be good to have the creep gone for a little while.

Heading inside to put the steaks and drinks in the refrigerator, he then located plates and the utensils he'd need for grilling, gathering them on the counter. After that, he moved toward the doors that led out back, where Kimberly was probably relaxing by the pool.

He walked out—and stopped dead in his tracks. Yep,

Kimberly was by the pool, all right. She lay there in glorious, sensuous abandon, her arms lifted over her head, her body stretched across the chair like a cat sunning itself.

He'd forgotten how good she looked in a bikini. This one was bold and floral in design, the colors vibrant beneath the bright sun. But he wasn't really looking at the bikini. He was looking at what was in it.

She was no twig—she had a perfect hourglass shape, slender but curvy, and every inch of her appeared incredibly touchable. His mind drifted back in time to what he knew about those curves, to how they felt in his hands. Touching her was like touching a work of art, her body a soft, malleable piece of sculpture.

He was getting hard again just watching her. But damn it, hadn't he just told himself this kind of crap had to stop? Hadn't he just realized that he was putting everything in jeopardy by letting his body take over his mind?

He ran one hand back through his hair and kept gaping at her. She was asleep, which somehow made this seem all the more bad. She didn't even know what she was doing to him—she was completely innocent.

And despite himself, it suddenly seemed that all the logic and reasoning and self-lecturing in the world wasn't gonna make the hardness in his shorts disappear. Like it or not, he was only flesh and blood. And she was…beyond tempting. *Just look at her. Perfection in the sun.*

And then he remembered how she always *burned* in

the sun, how she never took the time to put on sunscreen, always so anxious to bask in the rays, to just soak it all up.

So he quietly padded to the small pool house across the way and let himself inside. Locating a vast array of sunscreen on a shelf near the door, so he chose a medium SPF, then exited the pool house without a plan.

As he crossed the vast patio toward her, he heard more logic and reasoning in his head. *Just give it to her. Just wake her up, fill her in on what she missed with Carlo, and give her the damn sunscreen.*

But inside he was trembling. Trembling with how badly he wanted to touch her. Trembling with wondering—would she welcome it, would she want it, too, his hands on her body?

Shit. He stopped, pausing in place, shutting his eyes.

Things were out of control here. How the hell had this happened?

But the answer didn't matter. What mattered was that he was way too turned on to push down his desire for her, way too turned on to do anything but *act on it*. He knew it was suicide, in more ways than he cared to acknowledge. But he couldn't keep himself from going to her, not even for one more second.

He strode the rest of the way across the patio and gazed down on her, all the heat in his veins making his entire body pulse with anticipation.

Then he kneeled next to her.

And he reached out to touch her.

Chapter Nine

IN KIMBERLY'S DREAM, Max was touching her.

His fingers drifted over her bare stomach, moving in slow wide circles. He was rubbing something—lotion—onto her, making her hot skin feel moist and slick beneath the sun's heat. It was a good dream.

She pulled in her breath with a slow hiss when he ventured farther down, moving his hand over her belly button and lower, to the edge of her bikini bottoms. She bit her lip when his fingertips slid inside. Oh yes, this was a *very* good dream.

But then he slid them back out and she suffered a small stab of disappointment as a wet dollop of lotion connected with her thigh, and she began to think sleepily, *Oh, what if this isn't a dream? What if Max is really touching…?*

She tried to grab on to the thought, but half-sleep kept her from thinking clearly, kept her from coming fully awake. Yet when she finally summoned the strength to ease her eyes open, she found…dear God, Max bending over her, applying suntan lotion to her legs.

"Oh," she breathed.

He looked up and their gazes met. But he didn't stop massaging the lotion—he worked it into her calf now, his touch deep and slow, like the penetrating caress of a lover.

"Didn't want you to burn," he whispered.

"Where is…"

"Not here."

"Oh, then it's…"

"Just you and me. For now."

"Mmm." She bit her lip as his fingers caressed deeply into her lower thigh, moving back up her leg. It felt so good. *Too* good.

"Close your eyes, babe," he murmured.

And she didn't argue or protest. She did what he asked. She closed her eyes. She let him keep touching her, and touching her, and touching her.

He used both hands, smoothing the lotion into her other leg now, down her thigh, over her knee, and onto her calf. Then he slid them warmly back up, still rubbing, massaging, making her tingle with heated desire as his sweet touch came higher, closer to where she longed for it.

He pulled away then, shifting his ministrations to a new place, beginning to rub lotion onto her shoulders and slowly down each arm. And Kimberly lay there drinking it all in, each sexy touch, each sliver of excitement that it injected into her soul.

Then his fingers were—oh!—near her neck, smoothing, pressing in small rhythmic circles, working their way down one strap of her bikini top, moving onto the exposed ridge of her breast, fingertips reaching just past the top's edge, sending her desire to a fever pitch. She bit her lip in response to the throbbing sensations below. She wanted him to touch her more, *everywhere*. Wanted him to slide one hand into her top, another into her bottoms. Wanted to move against him and seek her pleasure and explode for him in wild release.

Her lips were quivering now. *Kiss me. Oh please, Max—kiss me.*

But Max—who had always been a slow and thorough lover—continued in the same pattern, his fingers now leaving the valley between her breasts and gliding up onto the curve of the other, and she bit her lip harder to keep from whimpering, to keep from begging him.

Her heart beat a frantic cadence when he moved his caresses back down her body, the cool lotion being smoothed into the skin at her hips, and the tops of her thighs. So close, so achingly near to the center of her desire. "Oh, Max…" She hadn't meant to utter it, but it had spilled from her lips with her escalating need.

"I didn't get around the edges of your suit before." He spoke in a husky timbre, making it clear to them both that this wasn't the real reason his touch lingered in that particular area.

She opened her eyes and their gazes connected.

"Should I stop, babe?"

She released a heavy breath she hadn't realized she

was holding. Then gave her head a short shake. An emphatic *no*.

And she watched as his dark, sexy eyes narrowed on her with a heat so intense it might have frightened her coming from anyone else. But it didn't frighten her with Max. *Nothing* frightened her with Max. She loved him. And she wanted him to touch her so badly she could taste it.

He slid the tips of his fingers beneath the thin strip of Lycra at her hip. She hissed in her breath again, wanting this sweet, horrible teasing to end, wanting him to touch her *there. Now.* "Max," she whispered. "Please."

Hearing his labored breath above her, she let her eyes fall shut. And she felt his fingertips moving, sliding ever-so-slowly, ever-so-hotly, getting nearer, nearer, until she wanted to scream. And she realized that she was gripping onto the arms of the chair as if holding on for dear life, and she was panting wildly, and then his strong fingers moved over and down through the small thatch of hair and slid warmly into—

His hand was suddenly gone.

"Damn," he said.

Her eyes bolted open and she raised her head. "Max?"

He stood above her, peering down. "I just heard a car door. He's back."

"Oh," she murmured on a sigh of utter disbelief. *He was back? How could this be? How could it happen?* She didn't even know where the hell Carlo had *gone*, why

Max had been here without him, but she still couldn't believe he was *back*—now, at this pivotal second in time.

They stared at each other for a long, awkward moment—thrust unpleasantly back to the reality of why they were here—and she longed to say something, anything, to make this seem less strange and uncomfortable, to make it seem normal and right. But she couldn't find any words.

"I'd...better go meet him," Max finally said. And then he was disappearing through the French doors, that quickly, leaving her alone. She sat up, blinking to hold back tears of frustration as she struggled to catch her breath.

Oh damn it, damn it, damn it! Now Carlo was here and the role-playing would begin again and she had to be ready for him, and she had to be tough, and she had to be that way *right now*.

But she'd be damned if they were both going to come out and find her lying here looking shaken and bereft and nervous. She'd be damned if she were going to let Carlo come upon her stretched out body and gawk at her and feel all the things she wanted to make only Max feel.

So she rose from the lounge chair and dove swiftly into the pool, praying for the cool water to drown all her exasperation.

"HERE YOU GO, babe. Medium well, just like you like

it." Max set a sizzling hot steak in front of Kimberly on one of the bright white round patio tables.

"Thanks," she said, returning his smile—although she wondered if that smile was real or fake. All the lines were getting blurred.

He hadn't had to ask how she wanted her steak. But considering what had happened just before Carlo had shown back up, she could hardly concentrate on how much she liked his remembering another detail about her. There were bigger things on her mind. Like Max himself, and everything so hot and masculine about him from head to toe—from the dark, sexy stubble on his jaw to his broad chest to the alluring bulge at the front of his swim trunks. And like the strange sensations that rushed through her still—passion tainted with embarrassment. Or was that embarrassment tainted with passion?

Temper that with the ghoulish feeling of having her breasts ogled by Carlo while she cut into her ribeye, and things got icky. She'd just figured out that it wasn't merely Carlo's blatant lust that bothered her—she'd dealt with men like him before, men who saw women as nothing more than sexual objects, as she suspected most women had on one occasion or another. It was dealing with *that* at the same time as she tried to deal with wanting *Max* that made things so hard. It was difficult putting up the tough wall of *un*emotion required to deal with guys like Carlo while she was immersed in her very *emotional* response to her ex-lover.

She gave her head a slight shake, trying to clear it of

the encounter they'd shared over the sunscreen. That was the last thing she'd have expected from Max at the moment, especially after last night, after he'd left the bed she slept in. What on earth did it mean? And good Lord—would it happen again?

"Pass the salt, will you please, Kimberly?" The request came from Carlo and the move required a long reach on her part, toward the other side of the table and then back to him. His eyes drank in her every move. *Pig*, she muttered inside as she handed it to him to watch him sprinkle only the tiniest bit of it on his food.

"So where did you run off to, Carlo?" she asked with a forced smile.

"My place," he replied, gaze intent upon her now. Though it kept shifting down to her bikini top cleavage even as she worked to maintain eye contact with him. "To pack a few clothes."

Max was quick to speak up from the grill, where he stood taking up the other two steaks. "Honey, I told Carlo how you suggested he stay the whole weekend."

Well, *that* was a surprise. Yet she kept her pleasant expression in place as she said, "You did, did you?"

"I was flattered by the invitation," Carlo said, saving Max from answering. "And when it comes from such a beautiful woman...well, how could I resist?"

And then, under the table, Carlo leaned his knee into hers. Oh, ugh. Ugh, ugh, ugh.

Her entire body instinctively froze up.

And instinct instantly urged her to shift her legs away

from him and toward Max, who was now taking a seat on the other side of her at the table—but she knew leaning her legs away would be the wrong move, casewise.

Unfortunately, casewise, it was time to start being a little more responsive to the suspect, a little more inviting. She'd not exactly been *un*responsive or *un*inviting up to this point, but if Carlo were to make his play anytime soon, she needed to start letting him know she liked him—a thought which nearly made her gag, but it was what the job called for. And she was more than ready, at this point, to be done with this slimeball, so it seemed like time to move things along.

Thus, disgusting as it was, she forced herself to leave her knees where they were. And she even managed to toss him a coy little smile. She didn't look at Max to see if he noticed, but she was glad he was there, just the same. And she was glad he'd be in the closet when Carlo tried to seduce her, too. She still didn't know what the sunscreen encounter had been about—or where it left them now—but she knew she needed Max's protection with this guy. And besides, he owed it to her. After all, it was him and his amorous attention that had her feeling so vulnerable right now.

She let Carlo's knees touch hers for two minutes, maybe more, then moved them. That was enough—a good, bold, teaser-type invitation. And it was all she could stand.

After she finished her meal, she lay her napkin on the

table and leaned back in her seat. She'd gotten a slight cramp in her neck, probably from falling asleep in the lounge chair earlier. Emotionally tired, sated from the large meal, and practically ready for another nap, she let her eyes fall shut as she slowly rolled her neck, trying to work out the kink.

Bad move.

"Here, let me help you with that." It was Carlo, of course, rising from his chair and moving behind her to massage her shoulders. "I took a class on this," he went on, "so I know just what to do to make it feel better." Wow. She'd completely forgotten—for a second anyway—what a blatant opportunist the little skunk was.

But she was a good P.I. She knew when to make a situation work for *her*, too—when to play up her role. "Thanks, Carlo. That feels *wonderful*." She let the last word drag out in a sensuous sort of way she knew he would appreciate. And she put up her little emotional wall that allowed her to be touched by the creep without needing to turn around and strangle him.

Yes, lead him on. Make him think you want him. Let's get this show on the road. Because the sooner this mission was accomplished, the sooner she could go home and get off this crazy roller coaster ride with Max once and for all.

Being around him again was incredible, but *so* confusing. And if anything was going to start back up between them, it would happen much easier after this case was through.

That was when she caught Max's gaze. He was staring at her, one elbow propped on the arm of his chair, his chin balanced on a loose fist. But as usual, she couldn't read his expression. Anyone else in the world—yes. She'd gotten much better at that sort of thing in their time apart—Frank had schooled her on it this past year. But not Max and those warm brown pools of his. They stayed as cloaked and mysterious to her as ever.

Still, she looked back, trying her hardest not to show *him* any emotion, either—trying not to show her confusion and frustration over what had happened earlier, trying not to show her disgust over being touched by this leech. They exchanged a blank yet serious stare for the length of Carlo's grating massage.

It was all Max could do to sit there acting normal while Carlo got touchy-feely with her. He hadn't liked it last night, either, but at least then she'd been wearing a little more clothing. He knew from very recent experience just how accessible her body was at the moment, just how easy it was to reach beneath the fabric. He hated having her in such an exposed position with this guy and not being able to intervene without blowing things.

He wanted to kick himself for giving into his wants when he'd come upon her sunning—and he wanted to kick himself even harder for having left them both so on the edge of ecstasy. *Man, what bad timing Carlo had.* The very air had been filled with an incredibly hot, steamy tension that had practically burned his hands while he'd touched her. She'd *wanted* his touches as much as he'd wanted to deliver them.

And at the moment, he kind of wanted to kill her for sitting there letting *Carlo* touch her so much, encouraging it with her little moans of pleasure, giggling when the jerk made a stupid joke.

But then he forced himself to remember. *It's her job, you idiot. A job you hired her for. A job you insisted she do well.*

And she was doing it well at the moment, all right. Gratingly so.

After all, did she really have to be *that* encouraging? Watching—even while he pretended to be oblivious—made Max's chest tighten.

So she really thought this guy was handsome? *Handsome?* Seemed crazy to Max, but he was a guy, so how would he know.

Still…handsome? *Compared to me?* he'd even been tempted to say. Now he was glad he hadn't.

And he might have started asking himself how he could account for all his feelings about this…if he hadn't been so busy holding Kimberly's gaze, trying to see what *she* was really feeling. At the moment, however, her expression was surprisingly masked, surprisingly unreadable—which bugged him more than he could understand.

HOURS LATER, MAX stood in the kitchen in his swim trunks, his back against the cooking island, arms crossed in front of him. He watched Kimberly moving around the room, putting things away, running food scraps through the disposal, scouring grilling utensils over the sink, all the while still in her sexy bikini, perky as hell. Carlo was upstairs showering, but that didn't diminish his annoyance. After all, she'd spent the whole afternoon flirting with the other man.

He cringed at the awful memory of her sitting on the edge of the pool while Carlo pulled on her ankle, trying to get her to come into the water with him. Before it was done, the asshole's hands had climbed up her calf to the back of her knee. She'd giggled the whole time, saying, "You'd better stop it, Carlo," although it had clearly been in jest. And he'd simply stood by watching, getting angrier with each passing minute.

Yes, it was the role she'd been hired to play. But did she have to make *him* look *so* deaf, dumb, and blind? And did she have to do that pretty, light-hearted little giggle *so damn often*?

And now here she was, still flitting around in her bikini inside the house with nothing on over it. Soon enough Carlo would be back down here and Max had the bad feeling that if he turned his back for a second, the guy would be all over her, and maybe inside that bikini, too. And sure, he was here to protect her, but in his opinion she needed to exercise a little self-preservation, as well.

Now she was putting away the plates she'd just taken from the dishwasher, reaching up into an overhead cabinet on her tiptoes, arching her back to make herself taller, sticking out her cute little ass in the process. A nice view. Too nice. One he was sure Carlo would enjoy if he were here.

Only when she closed the cabinet door and looked around for her next chore did she finally notice his disgruntled look. "What's wrong?"

"Maybe you should put some more clothes on," he replied evenly.

The words took Kimberly aback and made her chest tighten. His tone implied that she was doing something wrong here. She refrained from responding—and instead gave him a look of warning that dared him to go on.

He took the dare. Although he kept his voice low. "I think it's safe to say the bikini has more than done its job with Carlo. You can cover yourself up a little better now."

Oh boy. Was he serious? She tried to keep from fuming inside, but it was hard to push it down. At this point in the game, she had no intention of taking any crap from him. But she kept her voice low as well when she said, "What's the problem here?"

"No problem," he said in a gruff whisper. "But I didn't exactly see why you had to let him paw you so damn much all damn day."

"Hmm, let's see," she replied, a sarcastic fingertip at her lip. "I'm supposed to make the guy think I want to have sex with him. I'm supposed to make him think I'm completely willing to be seduced. And so I didn't run screaming from him when he started to touch me. Silly me, what *could* I have been thinking?"

He narrowed his eyes in response to her sarcasm. "I hadn't envisioned it including a lot of touching, that's all."

She let her own eyes go wide "Are you kidding? You didn't envision touching?" She planted her fists on her hips. "Well, for someone who didn't envision touching, you've certainly been *doing* enough of it. In fact, I was beginning to think that was my sole purpose here—to be touched and fondled by any man within reach."

He took a step toward her, dark eyes narrowed. "What's that supposed to mean?"

She let out a breath of utter disbelief. He was actually going to act as if he didn't know what she was talking about? "Well, in case you weren't paying attention, Carlo's not the only man in this house who's had trouble keeping his hands off me. After all, what was that kiss you gave me at the door last night?"

He stiffened. "That was professional. To help him view you in a sexual light."

"Oh, and then what was that at the pool today when he wasn't even around?"

He gave his head a sharp tilt, his expression shifting from one of anger to bitter honesty—before he said bluntly, "That? That was blatant lust, Kimberly."

Chapter Ten

Lust. Somehow the word halted her in place. Because it stung—deep. Deeper than it should have.

She knew lust—she lusted for him, too. But what she felt for him went deeper than that. She loved him. And she knew he didn't love her back, knew too much had happened for him to *ever* love her, but lust, at the moment, sounded so empty. And despite herself, it hurt. So she said nothing, only blinked to make sure she didn't start to cry.

"What the hell am I supposed to feel here?" he boomed at her then. "First last night, seeing you in that dress—"

"You told me to look that way!"

"You're right, I did. But I sure didn't tell you to come to bed wearing a tiny see-through nightgown. And then today, that bikini. I know, you're supposed to wear that, too. But seeing so much of your body just finally got to me, all right? It was unprofessional and I know it. So sue me. But it takes two to tango, doesn't it? You weren't exactly fighting me off, were you?"

Oh, so he was turning this back on her? She'd heard enough. "Well, don't worry, *that* won't happen again—you can bet on it." Then she shook her head. "I can't wait until we're done with this stupid job."

"That makes two of us," he groused.

She shot him a pointed look. "Then I suggest we move ahead full-steam-ahead with the plan—I think it's high time you plant yourself in that closet and let me invite him to see my jewels. The sooner the better, don't you think?" She ended with a concise nod.

Yet he hesitated. And she didn't like the look on his face. "Actually, I haven't had a chance to tell you this, but…"

"But what?"

"But we're holding off on that until tomorrow. That's why I invited him to stay the whole weekend."

She blinked her disbelief as a tired sigh left her. "You're kidding. I thought that was just to make him think I was into him."

"Well, it served that purpose, too. But timing is critical here, Brandt, and I'm tuning in to the fact that he likes all this posturing, likes hanging around with us and taking his time about it. Rush it too fast and we could blow it. And I'm not taking that chance. So we're giving him a little longer to have his fun with us—and only when I feel the moment is right will I get that fake call from the office."

Kimberly just stood there, dumbfounded. "That's a

terrible idea."

His eyebrows shot up. "A terrible idea for catching this thief? Or a terrible idea for you and me?"

"The second one. Because I officially don't want to be around you anymore."

His full mouth pressed into a flat line. "Well, afraid the case is what's more important here—so guess you'll just have to tough it out and show me exactly how professional you can be."

"Likewise, Tate. Because this time around, you're the one who dropped his professional guard, not me."

And with that, she turned and stalked away from him, out of the kitchen and down the massive hall.

So he lusted for her. And he thought what she felt for him was a simple matter of lust, as well—a matter of two bodies drawn to each other by something as meaningless as chemistry. She entered the bathroom, shut the door, and let herself cry a little, hating herself for the weakness of tears even as she set them free.

But enough of that. Too much, in fact. She reached for a tissue and blotted her eyes dry, then looked at herself in the mirror. How dare Max Tate hire her to be sexy and then criticize and judge her for it.

Well, this would end *now*. She'd change out of her bathing suit as soon as she exited the bathroom. And she would wear a potato sack to bed tonight if she had to before she'd put on another of the sexy nighties she'd unwittingly packed. She'd do nothing to tempt him that wasn't completely necessary to the role. She'd do this job, catch this creep, collect her pay, and be gone.

She'd started thinking that being back around Max was wonderful—enticing, invigorating, tempting—but she'd been wrong. It was painful, and she wanted it to end as soon as possible.

Tossing away the tissue with a sniff, she put back on her tough P.I.'s stance and came back out, ready to be in character if she confronted Carlo. Then she made her way to the grand stairway and up to the master suite, ready to change into something Max might find more acceptable now that he was suddenly the clothing police.

COMING BACK DOWNSTAIRS in a short, shape-flattering, but amply covering yellow summer dress, Kimberly was met by Max and informed that their "guest" was sitting out on the patio enjoying what remained of the day's sun. Then he grabbed her hand and led her down the hall to the office, shutting the door behind them.

At first she feared he was going to continue berating her about her bikini, or perhaps find fault in what she wore now despite that it was the most conservative thing she'd brought. But instead he turned to face her, leaning back against the desk in a stylish button-down shirt and a well-fitting pair of blue jeans that were unfortunately snug in all the right places, to say, "Let's talk strategy."

"All right." She herself was more than eager to talk strategy at this point—it seemed the only safe subject between them. And she didn't really want to be noticing the viscerally appealing bulge in those jeans of his, either.

"I told Carlo I wanted to take you both out for a casual dinner tonight. I saw a little bistro that looked nice when we were out earlier. I figured I'd use the dinner as a chance to try to find out more about him. He's pretty tight-lipped about himself, but maybe we can get something. We might also consider bringing up the jewelry again. Maybe we can wheedle some hint about where he's stashing or selling what he steals. A longshot, but worth a try."

She kept her response simple. "Okay. I'll follow your lead."

"After that, we'll just be biding our time—likely until tomorrow afternoon, when I'll pretend to get a call from my office about some stock market emergency."

"Max," she pointed out, "there can't be any stock emergency on a Sunday—the market is closed."

"It'll be Monday in Australia," he replied, "and I'm an international sort of guy. Besides, I don't think Carlo's gonna argue about a chance to get you alone."

The very idea of that made Kimberly shiver inside, but it had been the goal all along so she wouldn't shrink from it now. And she also knew she wouldn't *really* be alone with him—Max would secretly be in the closet. Besides, she was tough and emotionless—all business. And she intended to keep it that way until this assignment was over. She was ready to take Carlo on.

"So then," she replied, "after your imaginary call, I'll keep Carlo busy on the patio or something while you go get set up in the closet?"

He nodded. "Right. The camera equipment is already there, so it shouldn't take long—give me five minutes or so and then you can come up. If Carlo doesn't suggest looking at your jewelry himself, offer to show it to him. And then we can bring this baby home."

"Sounds good," she said.

"Any questions about your end of this?"

"I just act submissive and passionate and let Carlo do the rest, right?"

"Right."

"And then when things heat up a little, I act like I've changed my mind. I decline his advances and rush from the room, leaving him alone with the jewelry?"

"Right again."

"And if things get out of hand, you'll be there."

"Right a third time."

She nodded, then turned to leave the office—when Max stopped her with, "Oh, and Brandt?"

She paused and glanced back at him. "Yeah?"

"At dinner, you can, uh, hold off on the touchy-feeling stuff. I think he's got the message that you don't mind him touching you."

Inside, her stomach roiled with anger, but she was a professional—an *unemotional* professional—so on the outside she worked to remain very calm. "Yeah, I already picked up on your feelings about that."

She started to go then, but instead looked back at him once more. "By the way, Tate, the next time you hire a woman to play this kind of role, you might want to spell out your expectations a little more clearly. You know, one touch by the pool, not two—that sort of thing. It's kind of hard to play by your rules when I don't know them." Okay, she was unemotional, but that didn't mean she couldn't make smart remarks.

After which she finally turned and walked out, heading down the hall toward the kitchen. She caught a glimpse of Carlo through the French doors, his back to them, so he hadn't seen her, thank goodness. She could use a few more minutes without the lout bothering her.

A few seconds later, Max caught up with her. "Looks like Carlo is content enough for the moment, so if we have a few minutes to kill," he said, "I might as well make use of it."

"How?"

"I'm gonna go search his room."

She cocked her head, caught off guard. "And what do you expect to find? The guy's only been there since last night."

"Possibly nothing. But you never know. A phone number of a contact, a matchbook from someplace he hangs out, some kind of clue to where the jewelry goes when it leaves the victims."

"A matchbook, Tate? Besides the fact that Carlo doesn't smoke, I'm pretty sure matchbooks went out of style as big clues for private eyes sometime in the last century."

He arched a challenging eyebrow in her direction.

"They were examples, Brandt."

She just shrugged, done trying to play nice with him.

"Your job," he pointed out, "is to keep him from coming in and surprising me."

At this she grimaced. "I'm not crazy about being alone with the doofus, you know."

"You probably won't have to be. Just stay here and keep an eye on him from a distance. If he comes inside, keep him occupied."

"But don't flirt or touch," she clarified. Adding sarcasm to the list of ways she could address Max that she deemed still qualified as being unemotional.

He just rolled his eyes. Then gave her a look. "You can handle it, right?" Challenging her again, the jerk.

"Of course." She rolled her own eyes in return.

She stationed herself at the table in the breakfast nook where she had a clear view of the back doors as Max headed upstairs. And she further pondered his instructions for dinner—no more touching. That was more than fine with her, but she was slightly afraid it might confuse Carlo. And what was Max's problem here, anyway? After all, if all he felt for her was lust, what difference did it make who touched her?

The French doors opened then, drawing her from her thoughts, and she looked up to see their smarmy houseguest. Pasting on a smile, she said, "Hi," sounding way more friendly than she felt. *See, you* are *a good P.I. Whether Max knows it yet or not. And yuck—wrong call, Max, because looks like I'm alone with him again.*

"Hi there, beautiful." Carlo walked up and gave her a thorough once-over, something she was beginning to think of as his trademark greeting. And he'd added the *beautiful* thing, raising the stakes a little when "her husband" wasn't there to hear it. "You look amazing—as usual."

"Well, thank you." She gazed at him from beneath flirtatiously slanted lashes. Then she stood up. "I don't know about you, but I'm starving. Max should join us any moment and then we can go."

"You know, actually," he said, "I need to make a phone call first in my room." And to her great astonishment—after all, he was not one to squander a moment alone with her—he headed toward the stairs. That fast.

"*Wait.*"

He stopped and looked back.

"Why don't you use Max's office down the hall? Quiet, private, and it'll save you the trip upstairs. Then I'll get Max and we'll be ready to go when you're done." She offered him a wide smile for good measure.

And he returned the wide smile, but he didn't go along with her suggestion. "That's okay. I need to get my shoes, too." Only then did she glance down and see that beneath his khaki trousers his feet were bare. Damn.

She considered her options. She could yell for Max. But Max hadn't *wanted* her to yell for him—he'd wanted her to keep Carlo occupied. And it might be a small thing, but she'd be damned if she would give him one more tiny bit of ammunition to hold over her head when he was busy accusing her of not being able to do her job.

Then an idea hit her. It was fairly lame, but so was Carlo, so maybe it would be okay. "Carlo, would you be a dear and do me a favor first?" This time she even fluttered her eyelashes, feeling a little desperate.

The request, thankfully, seemed to abate his hurry. "For you, gorgeous, anything."

She giggled for him, having picked up on the fact that he liked the dumb-girlishness of the sound, and then shifted her gaze to a philodendron in a ceramic planter situated on a high ledge in the family room. "I've been sitting here trying to figure out how I could get that plant down to re-pot it, but I just don't think I can reach it." For added effect, she threw in, "I've been asking Mrs. Leland to get it down for weeks, but she keeps forgetting."

"You do that sort of thing yourself?" Carlo asked.

She blinked, slightly caught off guard. A tactical error. Carlo had apparently been stealing jewelry from the sort of rich people who wouldn't be caught dead with their hands in dirt.

"It's a hobby," she claimed. "I...like the way the potting soil feels. Between my fingers. I like to...you know, just touch things. *Lots* of different things. Don't you?" She hoped like hell this was sounding sexy rather than just messy.

The tilt of his blond head came with a suggestive grin. "So you like...getting dirty sometimes, huh?"

Oh boy. "Doesn't everyone?" She giggled some

more. Then decided it was time to refocus on the pot. "And the poor plant needs some attention. So do you think you could help me?"

He looked up at it. "Well, I can try..."

And she understood his hesitation. The ledge was clearly too tall for *him*, as well. She wondered vaguely how *anyone* could get the plant down, or even water it. "I'll bet if you balanced on the back of the sofa you might be able to reach it. I'd be indebted. Will you try for me?"

"Of course," he said, back in full flirt mode. "Like I said, anything for you."

She watched as Carlo approached the couch and stepped up onto the cushions. And hell, this wasn't going to work—she could see that immediately. He was nowhere near being able to reach the plant.

And that made her panic a little. There wasn't much else she could do to occupy him without more flirting that might lead to more touching—with Max not around to keep him in check. And what was taking Max so damn long anyway? She was starting to feel kind of abandoned down here, so...much as she hated to, she pulled the plug on "occupying" Carlo. "You know," she said, "We have a little retractable ladder thingy in one of the upstairs closets. I'll just run up and get it for you."

And then she scurried away and up the stairs and straight into Carlo's room as quick as she could. She found Max bent over a bedside table going through Carlo's wallet—and he looked up at her like a man who'd been caught stealing jewelry. "What are you doing—trying to shave a few years off my life?"

She kept her voice low. "We need to get out of here. He might wait for downstairs a minute longer—but he's dead set on coming up to his room. There's nothing I could do to prevent it."

Max took a step toward her, looking completely irritated. "What happened to keeping him occupied?"

"I did all I could. And doing more didn't seem prudent given the circumstances. Now, if you'll just quit arguing and—"

Dropping the wallet, he took a step closer and clamped a hand over her mouth, silencing her. And then they both heard it—the faint but distinct sound of footsteps padding down the hall. "Damn it," he muttered below his breath.

It was too late to get out now.

So she scanned the room and said, "The closet."

Chapter Eleven

MAX MOVED BRISKLY toward the closet and opened the sliding door, stepping inside. Then he grabbed Kimberly's wrist and pulled her in with him, although it was close quarters, the move crushing their bodies together. Apparently the house's owners used this space for storage as it was crammed with boxes and garment bags.

A murmured curse left him as he attempted to find a more comfortable position behind her. "Try turning around," he whispered, so she did, plastering her back against his front. He slid the door shut just before they heard Carlo enter the room.

Max stood statue still, waiting for something to happen. Two things promptly did. He heard Carlo puttering around. And Kimberly shifted her weight from one foot to the other, moving against his torso in the process.

And he was getting aroused. That quickly. Jesus. His erection pressed into her bottom through their clothing.

He wanted to bang his head against the wall. *Somebody put me out of my misery.* Why couldn't he stop this?

He'd as much as blamed her earlier, but the fault was all his. His and his uncontrollable desire for her. And how could he be getting so hard *now*, while they were hiding in the closet, while they were in direct danger of being discovered? This was not the time to lose control of himself again—and considering that their bodies were practically cemented together, there was nothing he could do to keep her from feeling it. Things were going quickly from bad to worse.

"This is Carlo," Max heard him say outside the closet. That puttering must have resulted in a phone call. "Yeah, you should see this place, man—out of this world."

Hmm, so someone else knew Carlo was here. That was a beginning—the start of a clue.

Which, by all rights, should have taken Max's mind off his pants and fully into his job, yet that didn't appear to be happening. What was going on down there didn't exactly seem to be a matter of the mind. He grew more and more rigid against Kimberly's soft bottom and wondered how much she felt it.

"They're loaded," Carlo said, and then he lowered his voice so that Max could just make out the next part. "Haven't seen most of the goods yet, but the husband has been talking them up like they're the crown jewels. Ought to be a hell of a heist."

Okay, this was big. Whoever Carlo was talking to knew he was here to steal jewelry. Did he have a partner in crime? *Keep talking, Carlo. Tell me what I need to know.*

Though at the same time, Max couldn't help thinking: *Get off the phone, Carlo, before one of us in here loses our balance and goes tumbling out the door—and before my preoccupation with my partner's body becomes any more obvious than it already must be.* He couldn't believe how much he wanted to touch her, even now.

"They asked me to stay the weekend—not sure if it'll stretch out any longer than that."

No, he more than wanted to touch her. He wanted to be inside her. He wanted to push up her skirt, yank down her panties, and bury himself deep, deep inside her.

"Oh man, the wife is incredible." Carlo had lowered his voice again, but kept talking. "All curves and legs. And pretty friendly, too. I don't think I'll have much of a problem with her."

Oh yeah you will, buddy. Lay another finger on her and you're a dead man.

But Carlo had one thing right. Incredible? Was she ever. At the moment, Max was wondering how he'd ever let her go in the first place—ruined career or no ruined career. And her beauty and her body were only two parts of the equation. She was smart. And she was funny. And she was passionate—oh God, was she ever passionate.

But then Max muttered a silent oath. Kimberly's passion was definitely the wrong thing to be thinking about right now. Still, a flash of memory—her on top of him on a rainy Sunday morning three years ago, making love to him until they were both weak—only increased his longing. Hell, that morning had been enough to make an L.A. guy appreciate some gray, stormy skies. And he knew she felt it now, that longing—it would be impossible for her not to.

All he could do was hold still against her and wait for Carlo to get off the phone and leave. And all he could do was keep on wanting her—more desperately with each passing second it seemed.

But when Carlo said, "Don't worry, boss," that was enough to catch Max's attention again. It was one thing to find out he wasn't working alone, but another to discover he wasn't even the guy in charge. "I've got it all under control. You'll have the stuff before you know it."

Max put his hand on Kimberly's shoulder, his way of saying silently: *Did you hear that?* But of course he was already touching her someplace else, too—this one not quite as innocent.

And big news or not, he decided that as soon as Carlo left the room, he wanted to pull Kimberly down onto the floor with him, let their limbs and bodies get completely entwined, and then he wanted to pound into her, hot and deep, until she screamed.

Not that he could really do any of that under the circumstances. But it was the fantasy invading his brain. *Come on, Carlo, get off the phone before I lose my remaining control, little as it may be.*

Kimberly took a deep breath and tried not to move. The slightest flinch or waver and she would feel him that much more, pressing into the cleft of her ass. And she would want him that much more.

She yearned to stomp her feet in frustration. *She wasn't going to feel this! She just wasn't!*

But she did.

It didn't matter what she'd told herself a little while ago about being a professional. And it didn't matter how angry Max made her with his irrational reactions. Despite her best intentions, it felt like an eternity since Max had touched her by the pool today. She hadn't fully let herself acknowledge the intensity of her own hunger—but now she needed him. She needed his touch. She needed his body pressing up against hers.

She currently *had* the second part.

And even as she knew how badly she desired it, it was killing her inside.

She wanted to cry at the way she ached for him. It wasn't fair! When would this job be over? When would she get Max Tate out of her system once and for all?

And then an overwhelming sadness hit her, even amid her wild longing.

Because she would probably *never* get Max out of her system. If three years hadn't been enough to do it, how many years would? She had the very scary feeling that she was going to be in love with him for the rest of her life and that there wasn't a damn thing she could do about it.

Oh God. Now she wanted to lean back against him even closer, wanted to be wrapped in his arms, wanted him to just hold her and let her savor these strange moments in case they were the last physical connection with him she would ever experience.

"All right then," Carlo said into the phone. "See you after I get what I came for." And concluding with a soft laugh, he hung up.

Even so, Kimberly bit her lower lip, still thinking far more about being pressed against Max than listening to Carlo. *Oh Max, Max—sweet, sexy Max.*

Well...he *could* be sweet when he wasn't being resentful. And he was *always* sexy. She sighed and again berated herself for the terrible mistake she'd made that day three years ago with Margaret Carpenter.

Outside the closet, Carlo could be heard moving around—putting his shoes on, she guessed. Then everything went quiet and she knew he was gone.

And inside, she and Max remained still. And she closed her eyes and did what she'd done before—savored the moment, savored the connection with this man she loved, this man who lusted for her, this man who could never love her back because he thought she'd betrayed him.

Finally, he whispered, "Well, I guess you'd better, uh, open the door now."

"Right," she whispered too gently, then slid the door to the left, admitting daylight from a window and ending the strange, forced intimacy they'd just shared.

Stepping away from him to exit the closet was more difficult than she'd imagined and left her feeling oddly empty, oddly alone. Still, she wasted no time before moving toward the door, tossing over her shoulder in a voice still far too breathy for her liking, "I'm gonna go freshen up. I'll meet you downstairs."

"Kimberly, wait."

The request stole her breath. She turned to face him, summoning the courage to cautiously meet his eyes.

"I'm…sorry about that," he said. "In the closet."

Oh God. She didn't want to talk about. She couldn't…*wouldn't*. "Sorry about what?" She shook her head lightly, feigned ignorance.

He blinked. "You know. About …"

But she only shook her head again. "No. I don't know. What?"

He sighed and now it was *his* turn to give his head a vague sort of shake. "Nothing. Never mind."

Good. "All right. I'll meet you downstairs in a minute."

And then she was out of the room and in their suite and in the bathroom, holding onto the counter and peering at her forlorn reflection in the mirror as a desperate question assaulted her. *How much longer can I do this?*

A FEW MINUTES later, she connected with Max at the bottom of the stairs. "Where is he?" she whispered.

"Back out by the pool," Max replied with a roll of his eyes in Carlo's general direction. "He *loves* that thing."

She simply nodded. And unwittingly relived the memory of Max's arousal pressing against her in the closet. Part of her wanted to leap on him. And part of her still wanted to cry. She prayed neither desire showed on her face.

"So how about that phone call?" Max said then, smiling. A real smile—honest and unguarded and without even a hint of malice. She adored that smile, and she had missed it—apparently more than she'd realized, because it warmed her heart nearly to bursting.

"Pretty insightful," she managed to choke out.

"So Carlo's just a middle man," he mused. "Possibly even low man in the operation."

"Sounded that way to me," she agreed.

"This explains why he's never been caught with any evidence." He continued to grin, and she smiled back at his sudden exuberance over this discovery—trying to be happy for him, happy for them *both* that they were making a little headway and discovering information the police hadn't.

But it was difficult to feel any *real* joy considering all the heartbreak and frustration she still suffered on the inside.

BY THE TIME they finally left for dinner with Carlo, she managed to feel a little better, a little more confident. She had to, after all—she had to be in character, and she still wanted to play her part perfectly and pull this off for

Max. Not just to show him she was a good P.I. now, but also because it was nice to see him happy.

It was only when they reached his Porsche that they realized they had a problem. It was a two-seater. "Hmm, this won't work, will it?" Max murmured, clearly trying to hide his troubled expression.

"How about taking the Mercedes?" Carlo suggested. The one he'd seen in the garage. The one that not only didn't belong to them, but that they also didn't have keys for.

"Uh, well ..." Max stammered.

And Kimberly rescued him with what she hoped wasn't too lame of an answer. "That's cute, honey, but you don't have to be embarrassed to tell Carlo the truth about the cars."

Max looked up at her, eyes half alight with hope but also with the silent question: *Where are you going with this?*

"The thing is," she said, turning to Carlo, "Max babies those cars to death. Only takes them out once or twice a year, and that's when we've checked the weather report to make sure there isn't a drop of rain in sight, and the route to make sure there's no dusty construction. And even then he won't park them in a parking lot where there are other cars—too afraid of getting a ding in the door. They're his hobby. Aren't they, Max?"

"Um, yeah." He nodded.

"You should see him, out here waxing them, polishing the dashboards. I think he dotes on them more than

I do my diamonds."

Max tossed her a glance, admiring the quick thinking. *Good girl, Kimberly.* Then he looked back to the other man. "So now that you know my little secret—and the Porsche here is just my everyday car—you wouldn't mind driving us to dinner, would you, Carlo?" he asked with a slightly embarrassed laugh. He even stepped up to slap Carlo on the back.

"Well, I'd love a ride in the Mercedes, but…what the hell." Carlo smiled. "Hop in."

The ride to the bistro in Carlo's late model Camaro was fairly uneventful except for the fact that Max cringed each time Carlo shifted gears because his hand got so close to Kimberly's perfect knees. She rode in the front, of course, and Max sat in back. But he kept a close eye on those knees—the perfection of which he'd never really noticed so much before right now.

Getting out of the car, Max decided to deter any touchy-feely plans Carlo might have for his "wife" by taking her hand on the way into the restaurant. She peered up at him, a flicker of surprise flashing through her gaze, but he gave her a quick wink and hoped she understood that he was just doing his part to keep Carlo's hands off her.

As a hostess escorted the trio to an umbrella-covered table on a stone patio that edged a wooded hillside, Max couldn't help thinking it would make for a pleasant evening if Carlo hadn't been here. His hunger for Kimberly in the closet hadn't exactly faded over the half hour since it had happened, and he could easily envision having a quiet dinner with her as dusk fell to night around them, their passion escalating with the decreased light.

He could imagine reaching out to touch her, first his hand on hers, then letting his fingers glide sensually up her arm in a whispery caress. They would read the need in each other's eyes until he'd say to her, low and slightly raspy, "Let's get out of here."

And they'd share a silent but sexually-charged ride to his place or to hers, their bodies both humming with heat along with the car, and then finally he'd get her alone and slowly strip that pretty little dress off and—

"Max?"

Her voice jolted him from the fantasy and he looked up to see that a waitress stood looking at him, poised to write down an order.

"Drinks," Kimberly informed him, enunciating like he was slow. "She's waiting to hear what you want to drink."

"Uh, bring me a beer. Whatever you have on tap." The waitress nodded and went on her way—and Max immediately realized he'd stepped out of character. Wealthy stockbroker Max Tate would have ordered wine or at the very least, an *imported* beer.

But Carlo, as usual, was too busy mooning at Kimberly to notice, leaving Max thankful he hadn't slipped up on anything more important. *Get hold of yourself, Tate, before you screw this thing up.*

Whatever was going on in his head for Kimberly was trouble, plain and simple. And when he caught her smile just then...damn, it actually felt like...well, like a little more than the lust he'd labeled it earlier. Because he couldn't deny feeling it in his gut just as much as in his pants, and lust was usually a very straightforward thing for him—a pants-only experience.

But then again, they had a history. Kind of a big one. So it made sense if lusting for her was a little more complicated. He shook his head. This was not what he needed. No way. *Just one more day, pal. Hang on for one more day and then you can go home and be done with this silly charade.*

After their drinks arrived and they ordered dinner, Max turned the conversation to something that might be useful, trying to casually wheedle out of Carlo anything about who else he knew in the city, who his friends were, what he did in his free time—but the guy wouldn't give an inch. He claimed he'd just moved here a few months ago and didn't know anybody.

"That's why it's such a pleasure to get to know you and Kimberly," he said. "I mean, I really appreciate you taking the time to educate me about the stock market, Max, but more than that, I'm grateful that you've opened your home to me this weekend, as well as allowed me the opportunity to get to know your lovely wife." And then, of course, he grinned lasciviously in her direction, because he couldn't seem to be in her presence for more than a few seconds without doing that.

Kimberly gave her pretty head a coquettish tilt, returning the smile, and Max's stomach tightened.

Then Carlo leaned toward her and said, "Oops. You have a little speck of something right..." he lifted a fingertip to the corner of her mouth, "...here."

She giggled in response and it all served to make Max go even crazier inside. He wanted to fly across the table and rip Carlo's arm from its socket. He knew it was simply some combination of ego combined with desire, but that didn't help the impulse.

Instead of flying across the table, though, he opted for a much calmer and more effective reaction. He, too, leaned forward and deftly slid his hand onto Kimberly's cheek, gently turning her face toward him.

Her eyes widened on him prettily, tonight looking as rich and green as the foliage beyond the patio, and he liked what he saw in her gaze. Despite all the ups and downs of the day, she still wanted him, just like she had by the pool. "What?" she whispered.

"Just, uh, checking to make sure Carlo got whatever it was." He'd spoken throatily, not by design but because that's just how his voice came out when he was touching her. He focused his gaze on her lush mouth.

"Don't worry," Carlo said. "I got it."

But for Max, Carlo wasn't even there anymore. There was only her perfect mouth, half open and delectable, and her perfect eyes, all wide and wanting.

He leaned forward to kiss her...slow, gentle, short, chaste—and electrifying.

Pulling back after, he drank in the weakness in her gaze, and the very sight shot a bolt of longing to his pants, arousing him all over again. He knew he shouldn't have indulged that urge, but damn him to hell, he had anyway.

How was he possibly going to stand this temptation for another whole day?

KIMBERLY FELT LIKE she'd been run over by a truck. This had been the longest day of her life.

At least on the day when she'd lost her job and Max at the same time, it had happened all at once, quickly. But this—*this* was a nightmare. Between Carlo's unwanted touches and Max's scintillating ones, her poor body didn't know *what* to feel. It was hard going from repulsion to desire and back again, *over* and *over* and *over*.

She bit her lip, remembering Max's kiss at dinner. What on earth had *that* been about? Was he trying to save her from Carlo or remind her that he thought she'd taken the touchy-feelies too far with their suspect? Or was it just more lust? *That, Kimberly, was blatant lust.* The words from earlier rang in her head, and they still hurt to remember. And yet, maybe lust was better than nothing. Even if he didn't love her, she couldn't deny that it excited her to know he still wanted her.

Alone in the master suite, she sat on the bed playing with the faux diamonds from the safe. This was actually the first easy chance she'd had to familiarize herself with the jewelry as Max had instructed her to when they'd first arrived. She'd left the two men sitting by the pool with glasses of wine a few minutes ago—dinner had yielded no new information on Carlo, but Max was still working at it. She, however, was more than ready to be off-duty, thankful for a precious bit of privacy.

She pulled extravagant necklaces and bracelets from the round box, enamored of their exquisite beauty—fakes or not—but almost too tired to concentrate on what she was doing. Still, she tried to examine them and commit them to memory, and she practiced working the clasps—admittedly a good idea on Max's part because some of them were unusual and took a little study to operate efficiently.

"Ouch," she bit off. Then she dropped the necklace in her hands to the pile that now streamed from the velvet box onto the comforter. Had she actually just pinched her finger in a necklace clasp? Obviously, she *was* too exhausted for this. Perhaps she'd take a break, get ready for bed, then look at them a little more before returning them to the safe.

She used a switch on the wall to dim the lights—even her eyes were tired, and besides, a bright moon shone through the balcony doors to gently illuminate the room. Then, reaching behind her to unzip her dress, she let it drop to her ankles, stepping free of it and her shoes at the same time before stashing them away in the closet.

She was well ready to retire for the night—God knew

she needed some serious sleep to recover from this day and get her wits about her for tomorrow—but first she needed to figure out what to wear to bed. And as she'd concluded earlier, no way would she be caught dead in any of her little nighties. Considering all that had happened today, Max would surely think she was trying to seduce him and she had no intention of even risking that.

For one thing, she refused to give him that kind of satisfaction. Considering how their relationship had ended so abruptly, she didn't want him to think she missed him or needed him as much as she still did—physically or otherwise.

And for another, she simply didn't think she could take it. Oh sure, she could *take it*. She'd *love* to *take it*. But afterward. She didn't know how she'd cope. Being close to him was hard enough, but to have sex with him... Even as she longed for it with every ounce of her being, she also knew it would be disastrous for her. She couldn't get that close to him again, have that ultimate connection with him again, only to say goodbye tomorrow when this was all over.

A knock came on the door. Oh drat—she wasn't ready yet. In fact, a quick look through her stuff had just confirmed what she already knew—she had nothing suitable to wear.

And then an idea hit her! Maybe she'd snoop through the stuff in the closet that *wasn't* hers—and maybe she'd find some nice full-length pajamas. Afterward, she'd wash and return them and no one would be the wiser.

Well, no time for that now. She was standing there in a pink lace bra and panties, and Max was at the door. He knocked again, impatiently this time, as if to remind her.

"Just a minute," she called. Then she took a quick scan of the closet until she spotted a short satin robe hanging on a hook behind the door. It was fairly slinky, but it would have to do—so she snatched it up and slipped it on, quickly cinching the tie in front. After all, if she was going to borrow things from the lady who lived here, why not start now?

Padding quickly to the door, she whisked it open, lest she make an impatient Max any more irritated with her than he usually was the last couple of days. "Sorry, but I was changing and couldn't find—"

And that was when Carlo stepped into the bedroom.

Chapter Twelve

———

KIMBERLY'S HEART POUNDED painfully in her chest. And she tried to smile but feared it came out looking more like the complete shock currently assailing her. Why on earth hadn't she said *who's there* first?

But it was too late to lament the mistake—she had to stay sharp, no matter how tired or unprepared for this she might be.

"Hi there." The clod wore a big, goofy grin.

"Hi." *Smile. Try to smile.*

"Hope I didn't catch you at a bad time, but—"

It was late, however, and smiles were getting hard to come by. "I'm sorry, but actually, you did."

Though her visitor didn't look the least bit discouraged. "I was hoping I could entice you into a nightcap."

Where's Max? She wanted to ask, but held her tongue—she didn't want Carlo to think she was intimidated by this situation.

Still, this was *not* the plan. Not the plan at all.

"You know, Carlo, I'm really tired and about to turn in. So I'll see you tomorrow—"

"Wow, look," he said then, completely ignoring her.

She followed his eyes to the jewelry that still lay strewn across the bed. Apparently, this was the one thing Carlo liked gaping at more than her. But even that didn't last for long—he quickly shifted his hungry gaze from the jewels back to her face, and then down at the silky little robe she wore.

He cast a flirtatious grin. "This is like kismet. Did you know I was coming?"

She swallowed nervously. This was bad. Really bad. Not only did he think she had the jewelry out because she wanted to show it to him, but he also thought she was wearing a tiny, sexy robe because she wanted to show *herself* to him. She supposed it was no wonder after her performance over the last twenty-four hours, but still—*this wasn't how things were supposed to go.*

"Have you seen Max?" she asked.

He shook his head, offering a lecherous smile. "Don't worry about Max, beautiful. He's not here."

Oh God. That was the last news she wanted to hear. It was just the two of them, no Max, no protection. And no video camera rolling. This was really, really bad.

But she could handle it. She *would* handle it. She was a trained professional, after all.

More teasing—she would simply consider this more teasing for the big oaf. She would show him the jewelry, then insist on putting it away. She would promise to give him a closer, longer look at it tomorrow and imply that it would include a closer, longer look at her, too. She hated to play it this way, but she didn't see that she had any other choice. To totally refuse his advances might make him hesitate tomorrow when they *wanted* him to steal the jewelry.

"Put it on for me," he said.

She lifted her gaze to him. Hid another nervous swallow. Smiled. "Put…what on for you?"

"Your jewelry. I want to see it on you."

"Oh Carlo—now? When I'm in a robe? That seems silly." She'd decided on a small attempt to dissuade him, but added a giggle to keep him happy.

In response, though, he stepped forward, closer to her. "Silly? For me to want to see these gorgeous jewels gracing your gorgeous neck, your gorgeous wrists? Come on, Kimberly, I want to see you in them." His voice held sex.

She tried not to hear that, though, as she took a step back, toward the bed, toward the jewels. She still didn't like doing this—not at all—but if she appeased him a bit, it would be easier to get him to leave, easier to promise there would be more tomorrow. Tomorrow, when Max would be in the closet and everything would be how it was supposed to be.

She plucked a flamboyant three-strand diamond choker from the velvet box, then immediately realized—damn it, she couldn't put it on herself without the aid of a mirror because the clasp was too complex and the piece too short to maneuver with any ease. Still, she attempted it anyway, opening the clasp, then putting the choker around her neck and trying to fasten it without seeing. She failed.

And Carlo immediately said, "Let me help you."

He stepped up and easily attached the ends of the choker behind her neck while she held up her hair. The touch of his fingers, the warmth of his breath on her neck, made her skin crawl. And when he'd finished and stepped away, she breathed a huge sigh of relief that he hadn't exploited the opportunity to take the touching any further.

"But wait," he said then as she turned to face him. "The bracelet, too."

Oh brother. That quickly, he'd noticed a matching bracelet lying on the bed. Kimberly sighed and reached for it, thankfully able to put this one on herself, even if it took a little one-handed coordination.

After which she turned back toward him again, just letting him look at her, feeling horribly on display, and horribly uncomfortable about this whole scenario. Where in the world was Max?

"Beautiful," Carlo said of the jewels. "Exquisite."

She still tried to smile, but it was getting harder all the time. Dear God, the little robe she wore over her bra and panties could fall open any second, and then what? Well, desperate times called for desperate measures. "I'm glad you like it, Carlo," she said. "And I'll tell you a secret. If you come back tomorrow, I'll put it *all* on for you. And I won't be wearing this silly robe with it, either. How would you like that?"

His eyes brightened. "Oh, I'd like that a lot."

"Good." Her smile came more naturally this time, since it appeared he was going to leave peacefully.

That was when Max appeared in the doorway across the room. *About time.*

His dark eyes instantly blazed with anger. "What the hell's going on here?"

Carlo swung to face him, his own gaze wide, his complexion suddenly ashen. "Look, this isn't like it seems, Max buddy. Honest."

"How is it, then?" Max took a menacing step forward.

"I was just, uh, taking a look at Kimberly's jewelry." Carlo's expression softened as he reminded his host, "You said I should, remember? Those pieces in particular fascinated me and I couldn't truly see how they looked without her putting them on."

"And as for why my wife is standing there with barely any clothes on?" His gaze narrowed on the other man.

But Kimberly took this one, at the same time trying to save her own skin. "Carlo knocked on the door while I was changing clothes, honey. I mistakenly thought it was you. Nothing to be alarmed about."

"Nothing to be alarmed about," Max repeated evenly, as if weighing her words, deciding if he believed them.

"Nothing happened, nothing at all," Carlo added. He help his hands up in front of him as if to wipe the whole situation away. "I would never betray your hospitality, Max. You've been so good to me, taken me into your home, given me your friendship, and I would never try to—try to…"

He finally gave up on finishing his pleas as Max stood looking back and forth between them, as if mulling it all over. Finally Max took a deep breath, let it back out. "All right then. Guess maybe I overreacted and that we can just chalk this up to bad timing. Let's just forget about it, okay?"

"Really?" Carlo asked, almost as if in disbelief. "Me and you, we're cool?"

Max nodded, looking more relaxed about it all now. "Sure. But…I think it's time we all say goodnight."

"You're right, it's late," Carlo agreed, heading toward the door. "Goodnight. And I'm sorry to have caused any…*confusion*."

Max waited patiently, his heart still beating double time in his chest, until the door closed—then he turned to face Kimberly. Dear God, she was lovely, the diamonds shimmering at her throat, the silk robe she wore gaping open just slightly, enough to reveal a shadowy bit of cleavage.

But at the moment, how good she looked was completely secondary to his anger.

"What were you doing? Are you crazy?" He kept his voice to a heated whisper. "We had a plan, a specific plan, and we had that plan for a reason, Brandt. Can't I depend on you to do anything the way it was planned?" And yes, it was a direct jab harkening back to the Carpenter case, but he didn't care—he was too mad to care right now. Even when he saw the rage flare in her eyes.

"For your information, I didn't go against your precious plan," she said, keeping her voice low, as well—even if it was filled with venom. "He just came in. I was changing clothes, there was a knock on the door, and I threw on this robe and opened it, expecting it to be you."

Max hoped she didn't think that was a good enough explanation. "So when it turned out to be him, you just thought 'let's have a practice run' and yanked open the safe for him?"

"Of course not! Before he arrived, I was practicing with the jewelry like you told me. He saw it and asked me to put it on. What was I supposed to do?"

"Try telling him 'some other time.' Like when I can be in the closet, damn it."

She let out a huff. "It wasn't that easy, Tate."

"What if he'd taken the jewelry, Brandt? What if he'd gotten away with it, without us getting it on video? What if …" Max had fully intended to go on berating her, but his next thought silenced him unexpectedly and came with the strangest sensation in his chest—like something inside him was shattering. "What if he'd…forced you to…without me here to stop him?"

He lifted his gaze back to hers then, taken aback to see how upset she looked as she mumbled, "What do you care, anyway?"

At this, Max took a deep breath, let it back out. He didn't think anyone had ever said anything so insulting to him in his entire life. "You might think I'm a Class A jerk, Brandt, but I'm not *that* bad a guy. You may have ruined my entire career once upon a time, but I don't hate you. You and I, we..." He ran a hand back through his hair. "Well, you should know me well enough to know I would never want anything bad to happen to you."

He'd said more than he'd planned—but still hadn't told her the way he *really* felt. At the moment, he was pretty sure he'd *die* if anything ever happened to her. And even though it wasn't his fault, he should have been there to protect her.

That was when one shiny tear rolled down her cheek in the moonlit room. The diamonds and the teardrop shimmered in startling contrast against her silken skin. And he hated that he'd made her cry. He hated it.

"That's always what it comes back to, isn't it?" she said in a voice so soft he barely recognized it. "Our history. Our past. What I did to you. You can't find a way to look beyond it. You can't even *try* to forgive me."

"Kimberly," he whispered, taking a step toward her, narrowing the gap between them, "you have to understand how I felt then. I had worked my whole life to get where I was—it was everything to me. To have the rug pulled out from under me like that, to lose it all in under two minutes flat—I was devastated."

"That's how you felt *then*," she said, peering cautiously up at him. "But how do you feel *now*?"

Good question. One Max didn't know the answer to.

So he didn't reply. He simply stepped up close to her, because the one thing he *did* know was that this was where he wanted to be—close to her. And he realized that her robe had come untied, falling open, and that whatever she wore underneath was scant and lacy and pale. He met her gaze, soft and without distinct color in the dim night air.

"Look how beautiful you are like this."

Her voice was barely audible. "Wh-what?"

"All dripping and shimmering with diamonds and tears. I'm sorry—sorry to make you cry." Then he attempted a gentle smile. "They look good on you." Although he felt the need to add, "The diamonds. Not the tears."

"They're fake," she reminded him, sniffing. "The diamonds. Not the tears."

"They're still beautiful. Especially beautiful on you, babe. What man could resist you?"

"You do pretty well," she muttered.

And he immediately shook his head, unable to believe she really thought that. "Not so well," he told her. "Have you forgotten already? My lust by the pool?"

He watched as she bit her lip. Maybe she *had* forgotten. But she was clearly remembering it now. He reached up to wipe a last solitary tear away with the back of his thumb. He didn't want to see anything on her face but the longing he knew she felt for him.

Lowering his hand to her hip inside the robe, his fingertips met with soft lace, his palm with her flesh—a mix of sensations that sent his desire skyrocketing. Then he indulged the urge to let his touch slide higher, moving it slowly up over the curve of her waist, stopping it next to her soft, full breast. "Did it feel good today by the pool, Kimberly? Me touching you."

"Yes," she whispered.

"Does *this* feel good?" He reached out his thumb to stroke her nipple through the lace of her bra. It beaded instantly.

"Yes." Her voice came out heated and trembling now.

And he knew he'd gone too far.

And he also knew he was just about to go much further.

He leaned close to her ear. "Let me do things to you, Kimberly. Let me take you to bed. Let me make you pant and moan and scream all night long."

Chapter Thirteen

IT HAD SEEMED like an eternity for Kimberly between the pool and the closet—now it seemed like an eternity since the closet and *this*. This, Max's hand on her aching breast. Max's raspy voice in her ear, whispering the hottest invitation she'd ever received.

She knew she should find the strength to say no. Because she knew, by his own admission, that all he felt for her was lust. But he'd weakened her defenses, bit by bit. Made her so weak and hungry. It was a horrible, wonderful culmination of all the emotions and sensations she'd experienced since seeing him again.

"Oh Max …" she breathed.

He was still near her ear, his warm breath branding her skin there. "Say yes, babe. Tell me you want me as much as I want you."

And she was *too* weak, *too* hungry, to turn him down. If lust was all she could have from him, she'd take it.

"Yes, Max, yes. I want you. You know I do."

A heavy sigh of blissful relief whooshed from him. And then he was lowering warm, soft kisses to her neck—just before raking his teeth gently down her earlobe. Oh my—she sucked in her breath as incredible sensation moved all through her, reaching places far beyond her ear.

His kisses moved to her mouth then—hot, delicate tongue kisses that seemed to wrap around her and take hold of her soul. He cupped both of her breasts in his hands and she gasped her pleasure—how badly she had yearned for this. For three long, lonely years she had waited, dreamed, of being in Max's arms again, and right now she wanted him more than she ever had before.

He kissed her some more—kissed her as he kneaded her breasts, kissed her as he pushed the silky robe off her shoulders and to the floor. He kissed her as he eased one hand down over her hip, then let it dip teasingly between her legs before brushing his fingertips up over her bare stomach, finally stopping at the front clasp on her bra.

As the clasp came undone, the bra loosening around her, she basked in the sensation of being undressed by him—even if she hadn't been wearing much in the first place. And then he was pushing the lace cups aside, grazing his palms over her taut, sensitive nipples, then holding her breasts in his hands, peering down at them. "So beautiful," he murmured.

He bent over her, raining tiny, fire-infused kisses to the tips, flicking his tongue expertly over the hardened beads until she feared he'd drive her completely out of her mind. After which he took the peak of her breast into his mouth, hard and fervent, making her pant and whimper, making her whisper heatedly, "Oh Max, it feels so good. Please don't stop. Please."

And then he stopped.

And she sort of wanted to kill him—but immediately she remembered. Max's lovemaking was legendary. He knew exactly what to do and when to do it. When she looked down into his eyes and he looked back, his gaze sultry and knowing, she knew she was at his mercy now and there was no taking control. She didn't even want to.

Sinking to his knees, he kissed his way down her stomach and she tingled hotly below, waiting, wanting.

And then came the sweet kisses on her thigh, edging upward with achingly slow precision—until finally they met with her panties. He knelt before her, gently moving the lace aside with rough fingertips, making her clench her fists and pull in her breath.

She watched as—oh God—he began to kiss her there, at the very crux of her desire, at the same time pushing two fingers up inside. She gasped, reaching over her head, clawing helplessly at the wall behind her so as not to collapse from the mind-crushing sensations.

"Max." She didn't know if she was whispering or screaming at this point, and she didn't care.

Using a strong, guiding hand, he lifted her left leg, placing her foot on a chair beside her, so he could reach her better, so that her delicate folds would open to him more. She clenched her teeth to keep from sobbing at how much she felt it, how his mouth was making her body tremble in ecstasy, how the sensations had now become wild pulses that rippled through her at lightning speed.

And it was about to happen, she knew, about to tear through her with all the power of a locomotive, about to bury her, and then…he was gone.

Rising up, he took her in his arms, where she whimpered, "Please Max, why?"

"Shhh," he soothed her, holding her close, dropping soft kisses on her neck, running his strong hands over the length of her back. "Don't worry, babe," he rasped. "We're not done yet. Not even close."

"But—" She'd been so on the edge, so deliciously near, and he—he'd abandoned her. "Maybe *you* weren't close, but *I* was."

"Shhhhh now. Trust me." And then he was kissing her again, those same passionate tongue kisses that turned her inside out, and she could taste the remnants of his affections, and on second thought, this hardly felt like abandonment. *Trust me.* She did. She would.

Pulling back from her, he gently lowered her panties to her ankles to let her step free of them. Then he stood back, gazing on her nakedness, until finally he uttered, "You take my breath away, Kimberly."

And then he was undressing, too, unbuttoning his shirt and nearly ripping it off, yanking the shoes from his feet, pushing his blue jeans down and off along with his boxer briefs. And she studied every contour of him, every masculine inch, just as he'd studied her—remembering, wanting. "Don't make me wait, Max."

His voice came as breathy as hers. "I don't think I can."

He dug in his wallet for a condom and they fell frantically to the bed, both shoving the jewelry aside, until finally he plunged into her welcoming flesh without a second's more delay. She tried not to cry out at how good it felt, at how right and perfect this seemed. He moved in her slow and deep, each stroke penetrating her very core, and she wrapped her legs around him tight, never wanting to let him leave her, never wanting this glorious connection to end. *I love you, Max. I love you, love you, love you.* Inside, she whispered the words, over and over.

When he pulled away from her yet again, she heard her own sob, followed by his soothing, "Shhhhh." And she felt like a terribly impatient lover, but she couldn't help how badly she needed him.

Then he rolled her onto her side, entering her from behind. She remembered telling him once that she could feel him deeper that way—and it was true, she still could, and a sharp moan escaped her with every thundering thrust. She'd never felt this whole in her life—this right, this incredibly fulfilled. Having Max inside her created a perfect moment in time, perfect beyond measure, and she prayed it would never end.

When his hand slid over her hip and thigh, and his fingers began to gently stroke her center, his touch was like velvet. She closed her eyes and let herself simply bask in it—until again that warm, driving tension began to build inside her, fill her, prod her, until she was grinding against his hand as he moved in her from the back.

And then it took her—a startling release. Stunning in its intensity, and beautiful because it was filled with all the love she felt for the man who had taken her there. Higher and higher the sensations carried her, until at least she was coming down, catching her breath, sighing her bliss.

Only he was coming now, too—with a deep groan as he thrust hard, hard, hard inside her. An overflow of emotion shook her at the connection they shared.

They stayed quiet, still, as he held her afterward, his arms wrapping around her from behind.

And she hoped he wouldn't notice her ridiculous reaction, but finally he leaned over, peering down at her in the moonlight. "Are you crying?" he whispered.

She lifted a hand to wipe her tears away and tried to cover a necessary sniffle. "No."

"It's all right if you are, Kimberly," he murmured, low and sweet. "It's okay." And then he lowered a gentle kiss to her cheek and lay back again, still holding her tight.

THE MORNING SUN urged Max's eyes open. Looked like another beautiful day outside—a beautiful day to catch a thief.

Then he glanced beside him in bed—and he saw Kimberly, bare but for the sheet that rose only to her waist, a diamond choker still circling her delicate neck. He crushed his eyes shut again. She looked incredibly lovely. But he'd made a very big mistake.

He couldn't believe he'd let it happen. Well, okay, maybe he could—it had started to seem inevitable as the day had progressed yesterday.

But it was completely unprofessional.

And it had clearly stirred up some old feelings for her, tender feelings—yet that didn't mean anything had changed.

The best thing he could do would be to get out of bed. Get in the shower, get dressed, get downstairs. Not make a big deal out of this. Move on.

So he rolled over away from her, ready to push the covers back—when she stirred next to him. Damn.

Peering over at her, he watched her eyes flutter open. Watched her turn to him with a sleepy, sexy, sweet-as-candy smile. "Morning," she said, her voice butterfly soft. Double-damn.

As soon as Kimberly saw him, her thoughts—practically her whole being—leapt to last night. To the complete and utter fulfillment he'd brought her, to the intense connection unlike anything she'd ever shared with anyone before.

"Uh, hi," he said, his gaze downcast. And only then did she really *see* him. The troubled expression shadowing his handsome face. The worry hanging over his dark eyes. His deep voice had sounded vaguely cool, dejected.

"Are you…okay?" she asked. But inside, she begged

him. *Please, please don't do this. Please don't act how I'm afraid you're going to act.*

"Yeah, fine," he replied without looking at her. Then he reached over the side of the bed and grabbed his underwear. "We'd better get moving. Big day today."

She sighed—looked like he *was* going to act that way. Like nothing had happened.

And she couldn't stand that. In fact, she *wouldn't* stand for it.

She sat up in bed and stared at him. "Are you just going to pretend we didn't have mind-blowing sex?"

Next to her, he sighed, but still didn't look at her. "We shouldn't have. It's my fault. I'm sorry. I got too close to you and lost control."

She swallowed hard. He'd just made everything completely clear to her. Even after last night, all he felt for her was lust. Still.

And she knew she should have foreseen this—in fact, she *had* foreseen it. She'd told herself over and over that to go to bed with Max would be a mistake because he would never return her feelings.

She'd forgotten about that last part amid her ecstasy—and now it was slapping her in the face, hard. And it hurt just as much as she'd imagined it would. Maybe more, because imagined hurt was nothing like *real* hurt. *Real* hurt cut to the quick and you couldn't dull it and you couldn't escape it. It was just a part of you. And already, it felt like the *biggest* part of her.

"I have a suggestion, Tate," she said, not looking at

him. "If Carlo's not around, stay away from me. That way you won't be tempted to lose control again." Then she got up and walked to the bathroom, slamming the door shut behind her.

MAX LOOKED AFTER her, immediately missing the sight of her pretty backside when she slammed the door. Apparently he'd handled this the wrong way. He hadn't meant to make her mad—he'd just thought it would be easier if they both got on with the business of doing this job.

He climbed out of bed and did his best to make it, fluffing the pillows and pulling the comforter up. Then he gathered the fake jewelry strewn around the covers and on the floor, and put it all neatly back into the black velvet box, which he also found on the carpet at the foot of the bed.

Of course, when he thought about it, she was right—he could try to pretend this hadn't happened, but it had. And he didn't think he'd be forgetting about it anytime soon. He could still feel her creamy breasts filling his hands, and the way her body had opened so warm and moist to take him inside. He could still feel the way his heart had seemed to contract when she held him tight, when her breath sounded so ragged in his ear, and when she came—*especially* when she came. Talk about evoking emotions—he'd felt things he didn't even know names for.

And then she'd cried. He'd almost forgotten that part until right now. She'd cried and he'd held her and he'd told her it was okay. He didn't even know what he'd meant by that.

Or maybe he did. Maybe he'd been saying: *It's okay to feel so much, because I feel it, too.*

Damn. It was true. He'd felt it, too.

He shook his head at the disarming realization, then grabbed up his clothes and went to use the shower down the hall.

KIMBERLY STOOD IN the shower letting the water cascade over her—hoping it would somehow wash away her mortification. But water couldn't do that. Nor could tears. She'd been having so many inane wishes lately—ever since Max Tate had re-entered her life.

Ugh, she couldn't stop remembering. How she'd begged him. How she'd whimpered and sobbed and panted and pleaded. He certainly wasn't the only one who'd lost control. Only her loss of control had been much more complete than his—hers included her body *and* her heart.

And good Lord—she'd been so overcome with love for him that she'd cried afterward? How utterly embarrassing. Especially now—now that she knew it meant nothing to him at all.

Toweling off with one of the plush bath sheets from the enormous linen closet, she promptly dropped it in the laundry chute and stood before the marble sinktop brushing her teeth. Plush bath sheets, marble sinktops—suddenly the lavishness of their accommodations no longer held the same awe for her that it had only a day or two ago. It just wasn't important compared to her feelings, compared to her heart.

After throwing on denim shorts and a T-shirt—who cared if Carlo thought it was sexy or not?—she scooped up the choker and bracelet she'd set on the sink and came out into the bedroom.

She'd heard the door close and knew Max was no longer there, but she was surprised to see he'd made the bed and cleaned up the jewelry. He'd left the black velvet box sitting neatly on the comforter, lid open, waiting for her to drop the missing items back inside.

Laying the gems back among the others, she gently closed the box, then slid it into the safe and shut the door. And she felt a distinct sadness fall over her, because packing up the jewelry and closing it away seemed somehow like...packing up her and Max's relationship and hiding it away, as well—which was obviously exactly what he wanted.

And that made sense, because the jewelry and the relationship had something else in common, too. Both were fake.

But snap out of it, Brandt. Toughen up—you've got a job to do today. You can cry your heart out later, but for now, it's back to work. And with that, she put on her tough investigator's face, tempered it with a little of the flirtation that came from Max's "wife," then went downstairs ready to put in this last few hours of work before calling it a day with him—forever.

Chapter Fourteen

MAX WASN'T MUCH of a cook. But he'd found some heat-and-serve sausage in the freezer and a bunch of eggs in the fridge, which he planned to scramble. He dug a big bowl from an overhead cabinet and began breaking the eggs into it. And he tried his damnedest not to let himself remember similar breakfasts on similar mornings, mornings after spending the night with Kimberly. After all, this was a lot different. He would be setting three plates.

Still, his thoughts swirled as he broke the eggs, one by one, and let the white shells plop into a garbage can. Because now he'd admitted to himself that he felt something for her. Something big.

And he wasn't ready for that—three plates or not.

Because there was a lot to take into consideration here. For one thing, the job. For another, the Carpenter case and all the loss that had come with it.

He turned the heat on under the skillet, then held his hand over it until he felt his palm warming. Kimberly had been right—he'd never really thought about forgiving her for the Carpenter case. But not because he was a rotten hard ass of a guy. It was because she'd never been around for him to forgive. She'd walked out of the room, and he'd gone to Vegas and spent the next two and a half years rebuilding his business. Forgiveness had never become an issue.

He mixed the eggs and milk with a fork, an array of questions wandering through his head. *Could* he forgive her? Could he forget? Where did trust come into play here? Did he really believe he could trust her now? In business? In pleasure? That was the part that had been so hard to take: Being betrayed by your partner was one thing—but being betrayed by your lover was much worse.

In one way, he felt like he didn't know her at all anymore—she was so much tougher and saucier now than she'd been then. But in another, he felt like he knew her completely, to her very core. And maybe somehow wanted to know her even better.

If only he could forget. And forgive. Forgive her for what she'd done, even if he didn't know why she'd done it. She'd tried to tell him the other day and he'd refused to listen. He had no desire to go back to that place, that time—to feel the betrayal and emptiness all over again.

Maybe he was afraid that whatever she said would never be enough to make him forgive *or* forget. Or…maybe he was afraid it would?

He dumped the egg mixture into the hot frying pan, surprised by his thoughts. *He wanted to know her even better.* Did he? Really? If anyone had asked him that three days ago, he'd have easily said no. But now things had changed. He'd spent some time with her, both as his pretend wife and also as Kimberly, the woman who had been his partner and his lover. It hit him suddenly that she was both of those things again—even if not by design. And as to the question of whether he could invite her back into his life again…well, it still all came back to forgiving and forgetting, two things he didn't know if he was capable of.

But first things first. First came the case. First came putting Carlo and his boss or bosses behind bars and getting his client's property back. And until that was over, he couldn't think about this stuff.

After turning the eggs with a fork, he flipped the sausages he'd put in another skillet, then shoved some bread into the toaster. As he got out three juice glasses, he looked up to see Kimberly walk in, wearing cut-offs and a tee.

"Hope I'm not too dressed down," she said.

He gave his head a short shake. "No, I think we've already got him where we want him. You look fine. Nice." In fact, she looked like the old Kimberly he remembered. That rainy day Kimberly. The let's-grab-a-quick-burger-and-catch-a-movie Kimberly. The easygoing girl he'd loved to be with, laugh with, watch TV with, do anything with. Go to bed with. He couldn't think of Kimberly back then without thinking about taking her to bed. They'd spent a lot of time in bed.

Which probably explained why last night had felt so much like…coming home.

Damn it. He shook his head. Hadn't he just told himself he couldn't think about that anymore right now?

"What?" she said in response to his expression.

"Nothing." He looked away. "Can you, um, pour the juice for me?" Then he started turning the eggs again, amazed he hadn't scorched them by neglecting them for so long.

"Sure."

"Any sign of him up there?" he asked, glancing her way. She was busy grabbing a glass container of orange juice from the fridge, and looking cute as hell in her shorts.

"I heard the hall shower."

"Good." Although this was no time to be thinking about Kimberly's shorts—he needed to concentrate on business. "I'll plan on getting my imaginary call from the office around two. Are you ready for this?" He met her eyes for that last part. It was necessary—he had to see how she reacted.

"More than." She sounded eager. *Looked* eager. Which was a good attitude for a P.I. Still, it suddenly bothered him. Which he tried to hide, but she saw it anyway.

"What's wrong, Tate?"

"Nothing." He turned his back to her, removing the scrambled eggs from the burner. And he realized that, to his unmitigated surprise, he was having second thoughts about sending her in with Carlo. He couldn't believe he'd be willing to scrap this whole setup, but suddenly he was.

"Brandt, this might be too dangerous." He still didn't look at her, instead spooning fluffy eggs into a glass bowl.

"Dangerous?" Even keeping his gaze down, he could almost feel her eyes widen in surprise.

"What if you can't hold him at bay?" he asked. "What if he gets rough?"

"I can handle it. And you'll be right in the closet, remember?"

He sighed and shook his head. "Still, I don't know. I'm not sure I like it."

She blinked. "You liked it fine before."

"That was then."

"Something change?"

It was as if she was daring him. To admit the sex had been more than sex, more than what he'd wanted or expected it to be. To admit that he worried for her, that he wanted to take care of her, protect her. And he remained just as unready to go there as he'd been five minutes ago. "No," he finally said.

"Then come on, Tate—toughen up. This isn't that big of a deal."

He looked over at her then, their eyes connecting, and their gazes held for a long, painfully slow moment. And he thanked God that she'd never been able to read his expression, or she'd see that he was having more of those damn tender emotions toward her again, that no matter how he tried, he was having a hard time pushing them into the background where they belonged.

"What smells so good?"

Max flinched and looked up—to see Carlo standing in the doorway. Although it appeared that he missed the look they'd been sharing. Showtime.

"Eggs," Max replied.

"And sausage," Kimberly added.

Carlo rubbed his hands together. "Mmm mmm—sounds great. I'm starving."

"Take a seat at the table," Max told the crook. Then turned back to the counter. "You, too, babe. I'll handle all this."

"So what's up for today?" Carlo asked as he sat down.

"Nothing special," Max said. "Have anything in mind?" *Like seducing my wife and stealing some jewelry maybe?*

"I could go for some more time by the pool."

That Carlo—he was a sucker for that particular luxury. Nice that the house had come with it—it made the lunkhead easy to entertain.

"Sounds good to me," Max said, lowering the food to the table and sliding into a chair himself. "You, babe?"

Their eyes met across the table—and he saw her slipping into character as she gave him a smile. "You know how I love to bask in the sun. Sounds wonderful." Then she shifted her smile to Carlo. Which Max hated. But he had to admit—she was good.

"Hey, Kimberly, watch this!"

Kimberly politely lifted her head from her lounge chair in time to see Carlo do a huge cannonball into the pool. *How mature.* She waited for him to surface and said, "That was a good one, Carlo."

"Something to drink from inside, babe?" Max asked from his seat at one of the patio tables.

Babe. She was trying not to let the old endearment make her feel anything, but it still did. Especially now, after last night. "A wine spritzer would be nice."

She'd been trying desperately to come to grips with what Max's actions had made clear—that he simply felt nothing for her beyond a sexual attraction. So inside she felt snappish toward him. *Quit smiling at me with those seductive brown eyes. And stop calling me babe.* Because none of that was helping her keep her hold on the reality of this situation.

And yet, she knew it was necessary. For the rest of the day they were husband and wife, whether or not the pretense broke her heart more with each passing second.

"Here you go, babe."

She opened her eyes to find Max holding out a festive glass covered with bright tropical fish, the spritzer fizzing inside. And he was smiling again. Damn him.

"Thanks." She reached up to take the glass with an obligatory return smile that nearly killed her. Because inside she wanted to cry. She might be completely capable of nailing Carlo to the wall, but that didn't mean she was immune to the emotions of unrequited love.

Her dainty fingers touched Max's as he passed her the glass—and something inside him tingled as he pulled his hand away. He gave his head a short shake to shrug off the sensation and hoped she hadn't noticed, hoped she didn't start wondering what was going on with him. Of course, he wondered that, too. This was getting worse, this thing with her.

To allay the feeling, he swung his gaze to where Carlo now sat dripping wet at the edge of the pool. Wouldn't hurt to do a little more digging, even if it led nowhere. "You know, Carlo," he said, "last night Kimberly was asking me where you were from and I realized that I didn't know, either."

Carlo smiled in reply. "Me? Oh, nowhere in particular. I've always moved around a lot."

"You have to be from somewhere," Max said with a friendly grin. If he could find out even that much about him, it could be a place to start looking into his background. Especially since random Internet searches came up dry. He still remained unsure about putting Kimberly in Carlo's hands up in the bedroom later. And if he had *anything* else to go on, it might help in his decision, even as irrational as his current thought process seemed—even to him.

"Nope, always just moved around," Carlo replied, cheerful as ever. "Even when I was a kid."

"Where do your parents live?"

"No parents," he replied simply.

From the corner of his eye, Max saw Kimberly sit up, adjusting the back of her lounge chair to the raised position. "No parents?" she asked.

Carlo shook his head. "Lost them both a couple years ago."

She tilted her head. "Oh, I'm sorry. What happened to them?"

"They were old, both of them in a rest home," he said, and left it at that, as if dying parents were a very small thing.

"I know it's hard to lose a parent," she replied. And at first Max thought she was trying to help coax information from the guy, but then her words really hit him.

"You've lost your parents?" Carlo asked her across the pool then.

She nodded. "My father died when I was little and I don't remember him. But my mom passed away just over two years ago. She had cancer."

Max swung his head around toward her—as she glanced away. He hoped Carlo hadn't noticed his shocked expression, but he couldn't hide it. When Max had known her before, her mother had been alive and well. He'd only met the woman a few times, but she'd been a nice lady, only in her fifties, and he knew Kimberly was close to her, being an only child.

"That was, um, two years ago in …?" he asked uncertainly. He felt like an idiot to have to pose such a question in front of Carlo, but he felt like an even bigger clod to be hearing the news like *this*, *now*, without being able to react.

"You remember, honey," she said, looking at him without really looking at him. "In April. Two years ago in April."

"That's right." Max didn't know what else to say. Inside, his heart was crumbling with sorrow for her and he wanted to show his concern, find out if she'd coped okay, do something to comfort her. But he couldn't—at least not right now.

He ran his hand back through his hair. Why hadn't she told him?

But, of course, when would she have?

Well, maybe when she'd asked about his parents on the ride here two mornings ago, if he'd only been civil enough to ask about hers in return. He couldn't believe it. What a devastating loss for her.

"I'm sorry, Kimberly," Carlo said. Carlo, of all people, comforting her when it should be *him* comforting her. He stifled a groan of frustration. "What kind of cancer did she have?"

"Breast cancer—that had spread to other parts of her body," she said, then swung her feet to the patio and stood up. "Time for a bathroom break."

Max watched her slender form move away from him and into the house. And he decided he had to talk to her—now.

"I'm gonna grab some snacks," he told Carlo, then followed after her—his partner, his lover, his "wife." Oddly, it was starting to feel like she was really all three of those things.

"Brandt!" he called after walking in the house.

"What?" she replied from the hallway.

"Wait up, I need to talk to you." He hurried through the kitchen and toward where she'd stopped just outside the bathroom. He stepped up close. Lowered his voice. "Why didn't you tell me?"

"Tell you what?"

"About your mother. I'm sorry, Kimberly. I can't imagine how hard that must have been for you."

She nodded, then glanced down, clearly uncomfortable with the topic. "Yeah—it was tough. But I got through it."

He nodded. His new, stronger Kimberly. Something about that strength made his stomach clench in a mixture of admiration and affection—yet also a little bit of fear. He only hoped the same sweet, gentle young woman he'd known before remained inside her, too.

He lifted a hand to her soft cheek, pinkened by the sun. "I just…wish you'd have told me. Wish I'd have known. I wish I could have…been there for you."

She shook her head, looking incredulous at his sincerity, and he supposed he understood why. It made him pull his hand back. "When would I have told you? We haven't exactly been in touch with you hating me and all. And you haven't been much for small talk this weekend."

She had him there. On all of it. He'd been heartless toward her. "You're right. I'm sorry."

"Don't apologize, Tate. We're here on a job, not to

socialize. But just don't expect to know every detail of my life." She looked him squarely in the eye. "I'm not the same girl you knew, Max."

"That's completely clear to me."

"Oh?"

"It's like you told me before. You're tougher."

Kimberly studied the handsome man before her. Was that a hint of appreciation in his eyes? Probably not. Since when could she read Max's always well-disguised expressions anyway? Still, she somehow got the impression he approved of who she'd become.

Now, she only wondered what he'd think to know that some parts of her remained as soft as ever underneath it all. That, in fact, sometimes she wondered if all this toughness she wore was truly genuine, really her—or if it was all just a complete fabrication to cover up her weaknesses. He'd likely be disappointed. But that hardly mattered—he didn't really care for her anyway.

Oh sure, maybe as a person—his concern right now over her mother's death demonstrated that. But it was a far cry from what she had going on in her heart for *him* and she knew it. So it was best not to start entertaining any thoughts to the contrary.

"And babe, I really am sorry about your mom." Lifting the same hand he'd used to touch her cheek, he now placed it on her shoulder, firm and comforting.

And at the moment she sort of wanted to collapse into his arms and quit being tough girl Kimberly.

But this was no time for that. Nor was this a man

who really wanted that. *Be the employee he's paying you to be. Pull away from him.*

Hard as it was to make herself do it, she shrugged free from his touch. "Thanks, Max." Though her voice had come out breathier than intended, and she felt uneasy—about everything—and suffered the urge to just get away. "You know, I think I've had enough sun for today. I'm going to go shower and change."

He nodded. "I'll go hang out with Carlo some more, maybe grill some hamburgers for lunch." He glanced at a clock down the hall, so she followed suit. It was noon. "Two o'clock will be here before long."

And thank God. The sooner this was all finally over, the better.

"You're…sure you're ready to go through with the plan?" he asked her.

"Damn it, yes!" she snapped, stomping her bare foot on the hardwood floor. When would he ever start trusting her to do her job?

"All right, all right," he said, raising his hands in a calming gesture. "Don't get mad."

"I'm not. I just want you to quit questioning me on it, that's all."

"Okay, Brandt, whatever you want. No more questions."

"Good."

KIMBERLY STEPPED OUT of the shower, refreshed in

body, but not in mind. She still hadn't managed to wash away the mounting pain of all she felt for Max but couldn't express.

Two more hours, though, and this would all be through. Two more hours and they'd have Carlo on film trying to steal her jewelry. She'd have proven herself to Max, once and for all. And then she could go home.

After which she could begin the business of trying to get over him again—which she knew from experience would be futile. She would always love Max, and her life would always feel less complete for not having him in it.

She toweled off in another of the thick bath sheets, then put on a short, summery dress that buttoned up the front, hugged her shape, and showed plenty of thigh and cleavage. She'd long since gotten bored with using her body to lure Carlo in—frankly, it hadn't taken much work—but most of the clothing she'd brought fell into that category. And besides, she had to wear something at least *sort of* sexy—since it was time for the "seduction" to finally come down.

She pulled her hair back from her face into a pretty chignon, then applied a little make-up, noticing the bit of tan she'd picked up the last couple of days and thinking she looked pretty in a summery sort of way. Maybe Max would, too. Not that it mattered, of course. His interest wouldn't go beyond her skin.

Well, back to work. Through the open balcony door, she could smell burgers on the grill. She'd go down in a few minutes, but first decided to test the combination and check out the jewelry again. After all, she'd gotten interrupted yesterday when she'd tried to do that. And in less than two hours it was showtime for real.

Padding across the carpet to the safe, she spun the combination. Thirty, thirty-one, thirty-two. *Voila.* It opened, and she reached inside to extract the black velvet box.

She'd seen it only hours ago, but something about it still managed to captivate her senses—as if the jewelry inside was real, as if everything about this weekend was real.

But it's only pretend. Remember that, Kimberly. Soon she would click her heels and be returned to the Kansas of her apartment, her real life, and all this would be nothing more than a dream. The only part that would count for anything would be putting Carlo Coletti—and hopefully his bosses, too—behind bars.

As she lifted the lid of the round black box to look inside, the reflected colors of the shimmery fake jewels danced in the sunlight that shone in from the balcony, catching her eye. The truth was—tough chick or not, saying goodbye to this weekend, and Max, forever, was going to be difficult, so for just a moment, she let herself get caught up in the wistful fantasy of it all, the best part, of course, being Max's wife.

"Kimberly."

The voice came from behind and caught her off guard.

Because it didn't belong to Max.

She tensed, then turned to see Carlo step into the room in his swim trunks and a T-shirt, a lecherous grin beaming from his smarmy face. He fixed a hungry gaze on her, then firmly shut the bedroom door.

Chapter Fifteen

ALL THE AIR drained from Kimberly's lungs. Her knees went weak, her throat dry.

But she forced a smile and tried to make it shine through her eyes as well. "Carlo, what are you doing up here?" *What do you think you're doing coming into my bedroom without even knocking? And what gives you the nerve to actually close the door?* But she kept *those* questions inside and held her smile steady.

And like it or not, she *had* flirted with the man. Openly. Repeatedly. That didn't give him the right—but with a guy like him…well, his twisted little brain probably *thought* it did.

"You promised to, uh, show me your jewelry today, remember? Looks like *you* were thinking about it, too." He glanced at the open velvet box in her hands. And his smile implied he really believed *that*, as well—he thought they were on the same page here and wanted the same thing.

"This…isn't really the best time, Carlo," she pointed out gently. Because Max wasn't in the closet running the video camera yet. And where the hell *was* Max, anyway? For a guy who saw himself as an ace P.I., he sure did lose track of the suspect a lot. Why did this keep happening?

"Why's that, sweetheart?" Carlo asked, his tone telling her the answer didn't matter and that he remained intent on getting his way.

"Well, Max is right downstairs," she pointed out anyway. "I thought we'd wait until later, that maybe I'd send him out to run some errands or something. Then you and I could have some…privacy." At this point she despised letting the sleazeball think she wanted anything to do with him sexually—but on the other hand, that was exactly what she was being paid to do here. And under the circumstances, it at least gave her a strategy to work with.

"Now, don't you worry about Max, honey," her unwanted guest insisted. "It's just you and me here."

Carlo had made similar statements before, but for some reason, this time it sent a fresh bolt of dread through her. He hadn't *done* anything to Max, had he? "Um, where *is* Max?" If he'd hurt Max, she would kill him. Brutally and without a shred of mercy.

"He's making us lunch," Carlo said. "See?" He walked out on the balcony, as if he owned the place, then motioned for her to follow. Her heart flooded with relief to find Max standing at the grill, now in a pair of khaki shorts and a golf shirt, flipping hamburgers.

"Well, don't you think he'll notice us missing?" she asked sensibly. "I mean, remember what happened the last time Max found you in here—he'll go ballistic. I wouldn't want anything bad to happen."

"I told him I was going to use his office to make some phone calls," Carlo said easily, stepping back inside. Then he chuckled and reached out, grabbing her hand.

Instinct kicked in before she could stop it, and she made a move to pull it back—but he didn't let go, his grip tight. Tight enough that her heart started beating double time, pounding like a drum against her ribs.

"What's wrong?" he asked with a teasing grin. "We both know you're into me. We both know you've been wanting this to happen."

"Well, not…like this," she said softly.

He tilted his head, trying to read her. "What's that supposed to mean?"

"I…I've never done anything like this before, Carlo—I've always been faithful," she said, trying to look bashful, emotional, like she simply needed him to be patient with her. *Get him on your side, convince him your way is better.* "So…this is big to me."

"Well then, come on, baby," he said, "and let's quit wasting time." And with one quick move, he yanked Kimberly to him, hard, making her drop the velvet box. Fake diamonds scattered across the carpet. So much for patience. She braced her hands on his chest and took a step back, trying to catch her breath.

What now? Break free of him and go running like a banshee from the room, screaming for Max? No, that would botch the whole assignment. And it would prove to Max that she really *couldn't* handle her job. She had to find a way to bail herself out of this mess and keep the charade intact.

"Carlo, wouldn't you rather wait until later when we could…relax? Have more time? Go more…slowly?" She had to stick to the flirtation—disgusting as that felt to her now. It was the only way. She even went so far as to let the fingers of her right hand walk teasingly up his chest. "Like I said, this is big to me. If I'm going to do this, I want it to be…thorough. Don't you?"

"Well, of course, honey," he said, sounding a little more reasonable. "I get where you're coming from. But—"

She cut him off. "I don't want to risk being interrupted and having to deal with an angry Max. I want us to have time to explore each other completely. I want you to…to make me forget Max ever existed." Ugh, saying that last part was like sacrilege to her aching heart, but it seemed like a possible way to Carlo's.

She felt sure this angle would work, because it had to—and yet he still pulled her back against him, tight. "Oh, don't worry, I'll make you forget any other man but me." Arrogant bastard. "And if slow and thorough is what you want…all right then, we'll wait a little while. But damn, girl, now you've got me all revved up—and you can't expect to get me worked up like this and then make me wait. So let's just have ourselves a little pre-game fun right now."

Damn it, all her ploys were backfiring.

And when he leaned boldly in to kiss her, feminine instinct got the best of her again, compelling her to turn her head away and push her hands against his chest hard, before she could even think about stopping herself.

But he still didn't release her and it was like being trapped in a vice. "What's wrong, baby?" he asked, laughing. "Don't play hard-to-get with me now. You've been hot for me since we laid eyes on each other. Hell, you just admitted it. So you're not leaving this room until you give me a little taste of what's to come."

Kimberly's stomach dropped like a stone. She was out of ideas, out of defenses.

And she suddenly didn't feel nearly as much like a tough P.I. as she did a very vulnerable woman who'd gotten herself into a very bad situation.

MAX HAD GROWN weary of making conversation with Carlo. Besides the fact that he never revealed anything about himself, he seldom had anything interesting to say. Other than gushing over Max's pretend life, he never added much to a discussion. So Max hadn't worked too hard at it the last few minutes—just letting the thief soak up the sun somewhere behind him on the patio while he kept to himself as he manned the grill.

Until he asked, "Carlo, how do you like your burgers? Well done? Medium?"

No answer.

So he peeked over his shoulder to where Carlo had been sunning by the pool just a moment ago. But damn it, he was gone.

And Kimberly was upstairs alone.

Letting the metal spatula in his hand clatter to the concrete, he ran across the patio and into the house, flinging the French doors wide. How had the little rat sneaked away so quietly? He raced through the living room and the foyer and took the stairs two at a time. Why hadn't he been paying closer attention, for God's sake?

He burst into the master suite out of breath, and just in time—to tear Carlo limb from limb. The other man held Kimberly in a forceful embrace—her hands were pressed flat against his chest as she leaned away from him as far as his grip would allow.

"Let go of her, Carlo!"

Kimberly gasped, then swung her gaze to where he stood in the doorway. "Max ..." The utterance sounded unplanned and desperate, her expression steeped in fear and something deeper he didn't have time to analyze—but he could feel her reaching out to him, needing him.

He shifted his eyes to her for only the briefest of seconds before darting them back to Carlo, enraged as a hungry tiger who'd just broken free of his cage. He clenched his fists so hard that his knuckles strained, filled with a fury so powerful he feared he might burst.

Crossing the room, he grabbed Carlo by the shirt and spun him around, leaving Kimberly to flee to the nearest corner, looking fearful of what would happen next. And maybe with good reason. Carlo hadn't actually done anything illegal yet, and if Max didn't find some way to rein in the anger that had taken hold of him, *he* might be the one going to prison.

"Max," Kimberly pleaded softly behind him.

"Come on now, man," Carlo was saying, his hands held out before him, "calm down."

But all Max could see was the desperation and loathing in Kimberly's eyes when he'd come in the room. He'd known he shouldn't let her go through with this and he'd been right. And now he finally understood why. *She* couldn't handle Carlo, and *he* couldn't handle *watching her* with Carlo. Both of them were too weak for the job, and even though their weaknesses lay in different areas, they had the same result.

Heedless of anything but his own wrath, Max pulled back his fist and landed it squarely on Carlo's left jaw. He wanted to kill the guy, wanted to make him suffer, not only for scaring Kimberly, but for each and every leer and touch he'd given her since the moment he'd walked in the door on Friday night.

Regaining his balance after the blow, Carlo drew back and threw an uppercut at him, but he dodged it and caught Carlo's wrist in his grip. His other fist slammed into Carlo's face again, knocking him backward into the wall.

Max didn't care about the case anymore—this wasn't worth it. It wasn't right that Kimberly, or any woman, should have to endure such mauling, even if it *was* for a good cause. Suddenly the cause wasn't good enough. *No* reason was good enough.

He closed in on Carlo, who stood cowering before him now, a surprised sort of panic invading his eyes. Clearly, he hadn't expected the "oblivious husband" to react this way—he'd probably felt pretty safe after Max had let him off the hook last night, in fact—and he probably hadn't pegged him as a guy who could fight. But as a P.I. who chose not to carry a gun, Max considered dexterity with his fists among the most essential of his skills.

The sight of Carlo looking so easily beaten did something to pacify him, though, to make him realize just how spineless of a man he was dealing with. Carlo was more than eager to prey on innocent women, but when it came to facing a man—someone of equal size and strength—he wasn't up to the challenge.

Their gazes met and held for a long, uneasy moment as Max waited to see the asshole's next move. He readied himself, just in case Carlo decided to come back at him. "What now, Carlo?" he asked, fists still clenched, eyes narrowed in threat. It was almost a dare.

Carlo's gaze darted past Max—to Kimberly, to the jewelry spread across the carpet, to the door—his eyes dancing with indecision.

But it appeared that the door won out. "I guess now I make my exit," Carlo said, inching toward it. Although a certain smoothness had returned to his voice upon realizing Max wasn't going to beat him to a pulp.

Max moved slowly after him, almost sorry Carlo didn't want another go at him. "Which is harder to leave behind, Carlo?" he asked, his voice still dripping with threat. "My wife or her jewelry?" And he knew he'd just come dangerously near to tipping their hand, but the words had tumbled out in anger. Pride demanded he not let Carlo leave without letting him know they were onto him.

Carlo backed into the doorway. "Your wife," he replied snidely, clearly not realizing the question was rhetorical. And then he turned a surprisingly smug gaze on Kimberly. "You don't know what you're missing, baby."

Max lunged for him, but if he'd intended to do Carlo real damage, he'd waited too long—the jerk had already slipped out the door and disappeared up the hall.

Instinct nearly made Max give chase, but several things kept him from it. Catching him would only mean pounding him into the ground—still a pleasing notion, but not particularly useful. And as unimportant as the case had seemed a minute ago, it still mattered, and Max was realizing he'd just made a fatal error. Somehow in the tussle with Carlo, he'd managed to get their positions turned around so that he'd stood between Carlo and the jewelry. Carlo had just darted from the room without it, so besides having nothing on film, they didn't even have any stolen jewelry to report.

But the biggest reason he didn't go chasing after Carlo in that moment was because it seemed much more vital to make sure Kimberly was okay. Max turned toward her, finding her lips pressed tight together, fists clenched at her sides, face painted with distress. He moved quickly to her. "Are you all right?" And he didn't wait for an answer before crushing her against him in a huge hug.

"Yeah," she murmured into his chest—and then she clung to him, letting her arms twine around his neck, and he held her as tight as he could.

Damn, it felt so good—safe—to have her in his arms where no one could hurt her, where no one could touch her but him. They stayed that way, and he forgot about everything else in the world except taking care of her—until a moment later Kimberly lifted her head and looked into his eyes to softly say, "Max, we have to go after him."

"What?" He'd been so lost in her that the words jarred him.

"It's our only chance to still catch him at something. Or at least see where he goes."

And...aw, hell. She was right. Giving chase hadn't seemed important when he knew Kimberly needed him, but she was a tough P.I., and a smart one, too, and even if they'd blown the jewel theft sky high, maybe they could still salvage some part of this case yet. After all, Carlo had a boss somewhere who was expecting some jewelry—with any luck, that's where he would head right now.

"Let's go," Max said.

And hand in hand, they ran down the stairs and out the door just in time to see Carlo's Camaro flying up the wooded drive that led from the house. When they hopped in Max's Porsche, he floored it.

"Hold on, babe," he told her. "This is gonna be a wild ride."

Chapter Sixteen

MAX BANGED HIS hand on the steering wheel as he drove. Damn it, he still couldn't believe this had happened—not any of it. He couldn't believe he'd let Carlo slink away and get his hands on Kimberly. And he also couldn't believe that after all the trouble they'd gone to, things hadn't come off as planned—the little creep had still managed to get away without doing anything illegal.

Max had thought the guy would lay back and let a flirtatious, assertive woman set the pace and issue the invitation, but he'd misjudged Carlo's ego. And he was a better P.I. than that—he should have had a back-up plan in place and kept a closer eye on the bastard. Damn all the distractions that kept making him mess up—distractions caused over and over again by Kimberly.

"Put your seat belt on," he snapped, glancing briefly over at her in her pretty little dress as he drove like a maniac trying to keep up with Carlo on the winding road.

Her scowl reached across the car at him as she fastened the belt, then said, "You need to put yours on, too."

He spared her only another quick glimpse before refocusing on the turns in front of him and the rear bumper of Carlo's car in the distance. "I'm a little busy right now."

"Then I'll help you."

"No, don't—"

But she was already reaching over him to grab the belt, and he was saying, "You're gonna make me wreck the car, Brandt," but he managed to get his left arm through the opening without killing them, and she finally got it snapped into place at his hip.

After which he murmured, "Thanks," because as irritated as he was by life itself at the moment, it had been a caring gesture.

The long chase led them across town and into a part of the Warehouse District that—despite some revitalization nearby—remained rife with old warehouses and deserted buildings. Many of the structures harbored broken windows—some that had been boarded up, others that hadn't. Holes and broken pavement pockmarked the street. Now *this*, he thought, finally makes sense. The Warehouse District had Carlo's name written all over it.

Max slowed his speed and hung back a bit—Carlo had suddenly slowed a little, too, since entering the rundown area. And apparently he had no idea he was being followed, the schmuck. It irritated Max to know

Carlo probably thought he and Kimberly were still back at the house lamenting what had happened, and it bugged him even more that he thought Kimberly had really been into him. It all just added to his determination to beat the guy at his own game.

"Look!" Kimberly said, pointing. Up ahead, Carlo had braked before one of the old brick warehouses and turned into the drive in front.

Max immediately pulled the Porsche to the side of the barren street, where they both watched in silence, although it was too far away to see much. Reaching under his seat, he snatched up a small pair of binoculars and peered through them.

"What do you see?"

"Looks like he's pulled up to a keypad, punching in a code to get him inside."

Then a large metal door lifted, and Carlo drove through, the door descending just as quickly behind him.

"Damn," Max muttered, lowering the binoculars.

"Damn what?" Kimberly asked. "We know where he goes now. This is probably where the kingpins of the business operate."

Sure, that much was good news, but Max shook his head anyway. "We don't have anything on them. Still no hard, tangible proof. I've gotta get something concrete, Brandt. If we have any chance of nailing Carlo and whoever his bosses are, I've gotta get inside that warehouse and take a look around, see what's going on."

She just gaped at him. "Are you crazy, Tate? We have

no idea what's behind those walls."

"And there's only way to find out."

He turned off the car and opened his door. But she kept staring at him like he'd lost his mind. "This isn't safe. I don't even know what you're planning, but I can tell you it's not safe."

"Wait here," he said. "And if I'm not back in half an hour, call in the cavalry—by which I mean Frank." He pressed the keys into her hand.

But she was shaking her head at him, vehemently now. "You're not going in there, Tate."

"Yes, I am."

She released a heavy sigh. "Well then, you're not going in there without *me*."

Max just looked at her. Kimberly. Sweet, brave Kimberly. Whose ability to handle this situation he wasn't so sure he trusted, even now. And whose heart seemed so big, bigger than he'd ever realized before.

He wanted to tell her there was no way in hell she was going inside that building with him. But they were partners on this case. She'd seen him through this far. If she really wanted to come, he didn't think he had any right to stop her.

"Are you sure you want to do that?" he asked.

"Completely."

He cast her one more sideways glance, and spoke quietly. "All right then. Let's go."

They got out of the car and walked up a cracked, neglected sidewalk toward the large building, hanging close to the other warehouses along the way just in case Carlo or anyone else was on the lookout from inside. When they grew closer, Max pointed out a single door at the corner of the structure near the freight door Carlo had entered.

Then he pulled his cell phone from the pocket of his khaki shorts. "I'm calling Frank," he said. "As a precaution."

A moment later, Frank's voicemail picked up, complete with soft blues music behind the friendly message delivered in a cool tone of voice. "Hi there. You've reached Frank Marsallis's personal line. Leave a message when the music ends."

"Frank, it's Max. It's Sunday afternoon, just after one o'clock. Kimberly and I have tailed our suspect to a building on Lang Street in the Warehouse District, with a faded sign that says Dormer and Sons over the door. We're going in to take a look around. I'll call you when we're out, but if you don't hear from me...well, just make sure you hear from me, okay?"

Disconnecting, he shoved the phone in his pocket—and began to have second thoughts about letting Kimberly go with him. A minute ago he'd been strictly in professional mode—thinking of Carlo and how to bring this operation down, thinking of the job and the life of a P.I. in general—which sometimes held danger. But this *definitely* held danger. And the more time he spent with Kimberly, the less he was able to keep *anything* about it professional.

He turned to her as they walked. "Are you absolutely certain you want to do this, Brandt?" Then he took a slightly different approach. "You might be of more use to me on the outside."

But she wasn't buying it. The challenging expression on her face told him so as she looked squarely into his eyes. "I'm a better P.I. than you think, Max," she said very quietly.

The claim inflicted a little guilt, catching him off guard. "Kimberly, despite the Carpenter case, I...think you're a fine P.I. Honest."

Kimberly pulled in her breath. He'd just called her by her first name, not her last. It shouldn't have affected her—it was normally something she took little notice of one way or the other—but at the moment, it pierced her heart just a little. Because yes, he'd called her by her name during certain intimate moments this weekend, and when faking things in Carlo's presence—but otherwise, he'd kept it all business in that way. Until just now.

Still, she didn't think he sounded or looked *truly* convinced. And maybe it was silly at this point, but she still suffered the burning urge to show him, prove to him, that she could work alongside him, doing the same job and doing it well. It was a matter of professional pride and it ran deep. In the beginning, he'd been her mentor and then she'd let him down. What had happened back at the house just now with Carlo had made her feel like she'd let him down again—she'd been unable to handle the situation, after all, and she'd been frighteningly close to crumbling. She had to make him see that she wouldn't let him down anymore.

"I intend to go, Tate."

He tilted his head and she waited for the argument she saw in his eyes—but then he merely sighed. "All right, Brandt. All right."

A minute later, his hand rested on the doorknob and she stood behind him, an eerie sense of danger biting into her spine. She'd told him back in the car that this was crazy, yet here she was doing it—she'd pretty much forced her way in on this, in fact—and it was too late to back out now.

Only when he turned to look at her did she realize how close they stood, and she fought back the impulse to reach out, touch him, cling to him. Because whether that was about fear or desire, this wasn't the time to let him see either.

"This would be a lot easier in the dark, but we don't have that luxury. Stay low," he cautioned. "When we get in, look for the nearest thing to hide behind and get there fast."

Her heart beat a wild rhythm as Max gently turned the doorknob—and voila, it opened with a barely audible click.

So when he took her hand, she welcomed the contact, the connection that provided a small sense of safety, the reminder that they were in this together. Then he led her into the enormous open-to-the-ceiling building where muffled voices could be heard somewhere, and guided her silently across the concrete floor until they could step behind a forklift that held a stack of wooden pallets.

She experienced no real measure of relief, though, until she stealthily peeked around to peer past the pallets and to see that no one had heard them, no one was rushing to see who had just come inside.

Then she turned to look at Max, who gave her a short, unexpected hug that quickened her pulse even as it reassured her. She'd done plenty of unusual work since joining the ranks as a P.I., but she'd never done anything like *this* before; she'd never done anything that made her feel as if she were in this deep.

Her only comfort was being in it with *him*. Despite her fears, she was glad she hadn't waited in the car—she would have gone crazy not knowing what was happening to him inside.

He took her hand back in his as they moved along the enormous outer wall of the building, thankfully barricaded by piles of crates and rows of steel drums. She studied the place as they made their way. It didn't look like the office of some grand jewelry thieving ring. It looked like a normal warehouse, dim of light and stacked with slatted wooden containers, the word *Fragile* stamped on their sides. Above her loomed aging rafters—from some hung bare lightbulbs dangling at the end of old wires.

Yet Carlo had come in here. What did it mean?

"Shipping," she suddenly whispered.

"What?" Max asked, just as soft.

"Carlo said he worked in shipping." She motioned to a stack of crates. "Maybe this is a legitimate business and he just works here."

Yet her companion looked skeptical. "I don't think so. He high-tailed it here too fast. And besides, I just have a funny feeling—call it a P.I.'s sixth sense—that we're extremely close to some answers."

Over the last few years, Kimberly had developed that same P.I.'s sense herself, and despite her suggestion, she agreed with him. In the distance, she still heard faint voices that reignited her fears, reminding her that they were in real danger from more people than just Carlo.

"What now?" she asked, voice still low.

"Now we investigate a little."

It sounded impossibly dangerous. "How?"

Max pointed to a nearby crate on the floor. It appeared neatly—and recently—packed, the top still open. "Let's see what these guys ship."

He silently reached inside and pulled out a heavy glass pitcher made of creamy white ceramic, the inside stuffed with wads of newspaper that would keep it from breaking in transit. Setting it aside, he dug through the straw in the crate, uncovering more of the same. But when he started to return the first pitcher to its place, they both heard the slight jiggle in the bottom of it.

Their gazes met briefly before Max reached inside, pulling out the newspaper. When he uncrumpled it, Kimberly fought to hold in her gasp—a ruby-studded necklace lay nestled within the newsprint.

"They must smuggle the stuff out in these things," Max whispered, "using the glassware as a front."

"What do we do with it?" she asked, her eyes still glued to the shimmering rubies.

Max hesitated, then stuffed both the newspaper and the necklace back inside the pitcher. "We leave it where we found it, for now. I'm not done investigating yet."

"But isn't this enough to take to the pol—"

He lifted two fingers to her lips, gently quieting her, eyes wide with warning—and she immediately understood why.

"Beautiful stuff, isn't it?" The voice belonged to Carlo.

Kimberly froze in dread, her chest going as tight as a rubber band—before realizing he wasn't talking to them.

He stood just beyond the crates they now crouched behind, speaking with another man. She raised up just enough to see several diamond necklaces dangling from the fingers of a paunchy, older guy next to him.

"Sure is," the paunchy man said. "The boss is gonna love it."

Carlo laughed. "Now you know the boss doesn't have an eye for this stuff—it's all just sparkly, shiny money to him."

The other man lowered his gravelly voice. "So, how'd *you* do this weekend?"

"Eh, not so well," Carlo said on a sigh. "Guy caught me messing with his wife and I had to split. And you know the boss's golden rule—never let anybody see you take it. Couldn't swing that this time, so I came away empty-handed."

Paunchy Man shook his head. "The boss ain't gonna like that, Coletti. Your little habit of playin' around with rich wives cost you a heist."

Carlo gave an arrogant shrug. "It's the first time I've ever messed up. The boss shouldn't have any complaints about me."

"So," Paunchy said, a toothy grin spreading across his face, "how *was* the woman?"

"Totally hot," Carlo said. "And totally crazy about me."

"How far did you get before you got caught?"

Carlo smiled. "All the way," he lied. "And even without any jewelry, it was well worth the effort."

The two men snickered and, next to her, Max went tense—so she instinctively squeezed his hand to calm him. He squeezed hers back, sending a small, warm charge of energy melting through her bones even in the midst of danger.

After chatting a minute more, the two men went their separates ways, leaving that part of the warehouse blessedly quiet again.

"What now?" Kimberly asked Max.

"We keep investigating."

"What else are we looking for? We already found some stolen jewelry. Isn't that enough?"

Yet Max sent her a reproachful glance. "Even if you

and I know what we've seen is stolen, we still don't have hard, cold proof. And I've come too far on this to leave anything to chance. But the door's right over there if you want to head back to the car." He pointed.

And she reminded herself: *Stay tough. Be the P.I. you know you can be. Do what it takes to solve this case and bring these crooks down once and for all.*

"I'm ready," she said staunchly beside him.

"Ready for what?"

"Ready to investigate. Ready to do whatever it takes to send these guys to jail."

He just blinked and looked at her, brows lifting.

"Don't look so shocked, Tate," she said. "It doesn't become you." Then she studied their surroundings. "Now, I'm thinking that door over there leads to an office of some kind. See the desk and filing cabinet through the glass? I don't think anyone's in there and it might be a good place to locate some paperwork that could be used as evidence, or for keeping stolen property before it's packed up and smuggled out. What do you think?"

A slow grin spread across his handsome face, and if she wasn't mistaken, she'd just impressed her boss. "I think you're right, Brandt."

Still holding hands, they cautiously made their way to the door she'd indicated—and after peeking around a barricade of steel drums, Max motioned her forward. She scurried silently to the door and turned the knob, her heart beating frantically, then slipped inside. He followed.

Together they began rifling through paperwork—she handling the cluttered beat-up old desk, he digging in the files. She wasn't even sure what she was looking for, so she only hoped she'd recognize it when she saw it.

And it wasn't long before Max stood at her side, silently pointing to a rumpled bill of lading clutched in his fist—and she saw the skewed numbers instantly. Someone had paid Dormer and Sons for fifty vases with over half a million dollars!

"Not all the invoices are like this," he whispered hurriedly. "Some of their business must be legit. The rest they must run through their system like this, pushing it off as extremely expensive glassware."

Their eyes met in triumph, then he folded the piece of paper and crammed it in his pocket, obviously ready to go to the police.

But then it occurred to Kimberly to wonder... "Crooks make out invoices for their stolen goods?"

Max shrugged. "I guess crooks need a way to track their profits just like anybody else, especially in an operation as big as this one appears to be. And laundering money makes an excessive amount of it a lot less noticeable. Now let's get out of here," he whispered.

They were making their way toward the office door when Max stumbled over a metal waste can, sending it toppling with a crash that echoed up from the concrete floor.

Going still as statues, their eyes shot to the tipped-over can before raising to each other. The noise had been too loud. And the timing couldn't have been worse—Kimberly could faintly detect voices coming from outside the office just beyond their view.

"Great stuff, Reggie," a deep-voiced man said. "Good work, as usual."

"Thanks, boss." It sounded like the paunchy man again.

"Boss, I just heard something." *This* voice, however, clearly belonged to *Carlo*.

And before she and Max could even move, the office door burst open, the three men looking in.

"Shit," Max said.

"You're about waist deep in it," Carlo replied.

Chapter Seventeen

CARLO STOOD BEFORE them with the paunchy man, Reggie, as well as an older guy who Max took to be the boss. The old man's craggy face spoke of age combined with experience—he was clearly a gangster, through and through.

"Who the hell *are* these people, Carlo?" he asked gruffly.

"These are the two I just spent the weekend with." Carlo looked Max squarely in the eye and shook his head, his voice deadly serious. "Maxxy boy, you made yourself a big mistake coming here. And bringing Kimberly?" He continued to shake his head. "Bad move, Max. Bad move."

Max didn't reply. But Carlo's words echoed in his heart—bringing Kimberly here had indeed been a monumentally bad move. And had he really managed to trip over a damn waste can? He sighed, worried and tired as hell—it didn't matter now. What mattered was that they'd been caught.

"I don't know why you followed me, Max—if you

were trying to play the big hero for your wife or what—but I can promise you this. You just got yourself in deeper trouble than you can even imagine."

"You know what to do, boys," the boss said then—and as Carlo and Reggie started toward them, Max's fight or flight instincts kicked in, and he knew this would probably require a little of both.

"Run, babe!" he said.

A few feet away, Kimberly picked up an old black telephone from the desk and flung it at Carlo, dinging him in the head and knocking him back a few steps. Meanwhile, Max found himself wrestling with Reggie, who—stronger than he looked—succeeded in knocking him backward onto the desk. But the position gave Max leverage and he managed to get to his feet even as he threw a right to Reggie's gut, then a left to his eye.

He saw his cell phone skitter across the floor amid the fight—just as he heard Kimberly's voice. "Back here, Tate!"

A quick glance over his shoulder revealed that she'd opened a door at the rear of the office, and if she was calling him toward it, it must be more than a closet. Reggie was recovering his balance now and Max just eluded his grasp, circling the desk and dashing through the door, which led back out into the warehouse through a pathway lined with steel drums.

"Run, Brandt—I'll catch up!" he yelled.

It took a few precious seconds and all the strength Max possessed, but he managed to haul down one of the large 55-gallon drums to send it rolling toward his pursuers. And after a few more steps, he brought a crate crashing down, too, shattering a mountain of dishes in the path.

Max's heart beat a mile a minute by the time he found Kimberly huddled behind yet another row of wooden containers.

"Don't make a sound," he warned her in a near-silent whisper.

Every nerve in Kimberly's body was tensed and ready for action. Daring to peek around the wall of crates that currently protected them, she spotted Carlo and the old boss man across the way. Now Carlo carried a gun.

"Find them!" the boss exploded. "Now!"

They hadn't been seen yet, but this was definitely not a good enough hiding place. Obviously thinking the same thing, Max's voice came in her ear in a barely discernible whisper. "As soon as the three of them get a little farther away, we make a run for it. Follow me."

She nodded.

Fortunately, their pursuers went in the opposite direction, and a moment later, Max said, "Let's go." After which they scurried quietly from their hiding place, ducking between another row of boxes and crates, passing behind a forklift, hand in hand.

That was when an announcement blared over unseen loudspeakers. "Attention. We have two trespassers on the premises. Find them and bring them to my office without delay!"

The voice belonged to the boss and the announcement meant there were more than just the three men in the building with them. Maybe a *lot* more. Maybe with a lot more guns. Shit—this was bad.

Max yanked her down the row of crates toward the other side of the warehouse until they reached the end of the aisle. When he cursed softly, she glanced up to see that more seedy-looking men had just appeared on the route ahead. A group of four stood conferring in a circle.

And before she and Max could even think about backtracking, they were spotted. "Hey, you there!"

At this, Max took off, dragging her frantically across the floor as she struggled to keep up. She had no idea where they were headed, and no other choice than to simply trust his instincts.

"Hold it!"

"Come back here!"

The voices behind her were close, too close, as she tried to keep up with Max.

"You can't get away, Max!" That voice belonged to Carlo.

And without warning, Max flung her aside and turned to face Carlo and his henchmen head on. "You want to make a bet!" He leapt behind a mountain of crates then and gave a mighty heave, sending them all falling before the encroaching men, blocking their path with a loud crash of splintering wood and breaking glass.

Then his hand was back in hers and they were running, running, until they came to a large steel door. He yanked it open and she went instantly heartsick to find that it wasn't an exit, but a large closet.

"In here," he said anyway.

She rushed in and he followed, shutting the big door behind them, leaving them in the dark. Inside, they both stayed quiet and stood close as their breathing began to slow. She couldn't help leaning into him, and he rested his back against the cinderblock wall and hugged her, warm and tight and long. No hug in her life had ever felt so comforting.

Outside, footsteps finally faded and gradually she began to feel that they were safe, at least for right now. Her heartbeat slowed as she began to relax for the first time since they'd come into this building.

And then Max's strong hands began to move, slow and still ever-so-comforting, roaming her shoulders and back. It felt too good to her, and she let her fingers curl slightly into his shirt as sensation trickled to her breasts, and then to her panties below.

But when he began to pull her closer, his caresses growing slightly deeper…when the only sound was that of their breath growing gently labored…Kimberly realized they were on the verge of descending into a desperate, slow-burning passion that could only escalate. As his touch skimmed deliciously over her hips and then higher, higher, his palms grazing the sides of her breasts, she came to her senses. "Max," she whispered.

"What?" he murmured, one hand stopping at the side of her breast, beginning to cup her there, his thumb stroking across her nipple, through her bra.

The exquisite sensation made her back arch as the juncture between her thighs spasmed. "Wh-what are you doing?" It came out too breathy.

His own voice sounded raspy, and sexy as hell. "Touching you."

Her response to him was impossible to push down—always had been, and that made protesting considerably harder, yet… "Max, are you crazy? Think about where we are. We've…we've got to figure out what to do."

With a slow, heavy sigh, he lowered his hand. "You're right. Damn—I'm sorry, babe. I was…a little out of my mind." He ran one hand back through his dark hair in the shadowy light that had gradually grown around them as her eyes adjusted.

"It's okay," she said, palms still at his chest. She could feel the beating of his heart "But we've gotta keep our heads here."

He nodded. And then they went silent—his grip suddenly tightening on her waist when voices could be heard again nearby.

"Where the hell could they be? They didn't just disappear into thin air."

"All the entrances are guarded, so they couldn't have gotten out."

The voices faded to obscurity nearly as quickly as they'd been detected, but the words Kimberly and Max had heard were enough to tell them they'd have to stay where they were—for who knew how long.

He released a heavy sigh and lifted a consoling hand to her cheek. "Looks like we may as well get comfortable, babe."

THE CLOSET WAS even larger than Max had realized—and was actually more of a storage room. Narrower at the front by the door, it widened in back, a compartment veering off to the left packed with boxes. He moved just enough of them so that he and Kimberly could barricade themselves behind them and be out of sight should anyone come in.

Now they sat side by side, their backs against the wall. Everything around them was quiet—but Max could only assume the place was being searched from top to bottom. While he held out hope for escape, he didn't feel great about their chances at this point.

"I'm sorry, Kimberly," he felt compelled to say.

She turned to look at him through the shadowy air, the only light that which seeped under the door. "Sorry? For what?"

"Sorry you're in this mess with me. Sorry I didn't make you stay outside. Sorry I kicked over that wastebasket."

"Let's get something straight here, Max. I'm in this mess with you because it's my job to be. I know you don't have much faith in me professionally, but there's nothing you could have done to make me wait for you outside."

There were things he wanted to say, things that lingered on the tip of his tongue and wanted to spill out. *I'm glad it's you I'm here with, babe. Good P.I., bad P.I., none of that matters now. I never allowed myself to miss you, but being with you these last two days have made me realize how much I did.* But he only sighed instead, maybe *still* not quite ready to admit the truth to himself—and then he reached out to take her hand. "Kimberly, tell me about…the Carpenter case."

Kimberly nearly went numb. He'd said it slowly, like it would be as hard for him to hear as it would be for her to tell—but he was giving her the chance now, the chance to finally explain what had happened on that ill-fated day.

She took a deep breath and tried to think where to begin.

"Well, I found out my mother was dying on the day I blew the case," she started. From the corner of her eye, she saw his gaze swing around to land on her, but she kept talking. "She called me around noon to tell me she'd been diagnosed with cancer, stage 4. She'd known something was wrong and had been seeing doctors and getting tested without telling me, because she didn't want me to worry. I wasn't supposed to meet with Margaret Carpenter until later that afternoon, so I was taking it easy in my apartment—letting her assume I was at work. So after the call, I rushed out the door to go be with Mom—and my cat got out into my building's common hallway."

"Misha?" Max said, stunning her once more by recalling a small detail about her life, even if it was only her cat's name.

She nodded. "I'd already locked my door, and I was frazzled and not thinking straight—but I saw my neighbor, Mrs. Baines, coming in, and she said she'd catch Misha and take her to her place. I figured I'd get her when I came home before going to meet Margaret. Nothing really mattered besides seeing my mom right then, you know?"

"Of course." He spoke quietly and squeezed her hand. And she tried to let it buoy her as she sank deeper into all the bad memories of that day.

"When I got to her house, we both cried and it was…well, rough is an understatement." She had to take a deep breath and steel herself to go on. "I wanted to stay with her and even thought about calling Margaret to reschedule, but Mom insisted I go on and do my job. So I headed home to change and when I got there—" her throat seized up, but she swallowed hard and forced the rest out, "—Misha was lying in the street. Dead."

"Aw, babe," he murmured.

It struck her funny that the memory of her dead cat came closer to causing tears now than the part about her mother, but—like then—it was the culmination of the events happening all at once that had the ability to make her feel so weak and helpless.

She took a deep breath and forged ahead. "Apparently, Mrs. Baines had trouble catching her—Misha was always afraid of strangers—and when one of the other tenants left the building, Misha ran out the door and got hit by a car. I picked her up and lay her on the sidewalk and cried until Mrs. Baines came out with a shoebox and helped me put Misha inside it. And then I pulled myself together and got ready to go meet Margaret."

Now Max was running his thumb lightly back and forth over the top of her hand. "You should have cancelled with her, Kimberly," he said sweetly.

"I know that now." She sighed. "Believe me, I know it. But at the time, I was on auto pilot—still reeling from the news about my mom and just pushing my way through the day, trying to get to the end of it, I guess.

"So I went to Margaret's house, ready to work. But Margaret...well, despite what she did, Max, she was a very sweet woman. She immediately saw that something was off and asked me what was wrong. I knew I shouldn't tell her, but I truly liked her, and I had to tell her *something*—and you always taught me that it's best to stick as close to the truth as possible when undercover. So I told her about my mother, and about what happened to Misha, too. Of course—" she stopped, rolled her eyes, "—I had to make up a stupid story about Misha being my friend's cat and not my own, or Misha would have been there with me at the bungalow. Having to lie in the middle of all that didn't help. But anyway, Margaret listened to me, and I knew she really cared, and it helped."

She paused again, readying herself for the next part— since this was the part Max had *really* asked her to tell him about. "Then her son came in."

"Our client," Max said.

She nodded, hardly caring about that fact. "I could tell immediately that Margaret was afraid of him. Like I'd told you before, he was gruff when he spoke to her. He didn't even knock on the door of her little house—just barged right in. And he ignored *me* completely. I was already so upset that seeing how he treated her made me angry.

"Margaret was clearly living on a shoestring, something I started thinking about while her son was there, and it helped me get back in a working frame of mind. After he left, I finally got down to business. I talked about the money she wanted to invest—and I casually asked her where she'd gotten it. She told me that she'd saved a little here, scrimped a little there. I said, 'Your son doesn't help you out with the bills?' And she said, 'No, I only have what I get from Edgar's social security.'

"And then—then I noticed these bruises on her arm, mainly because they were like fingerprints, like someone had grabbed her too hard. I asked her about them. And she blushed and looked away and started fiddling with the doily on the table next to her. When I pressed her for an answer, she finally admitted that her son had done it. She told me they'd argued and he'd pushed her. She tried to play it off like it was no big deal, but I couldn't see it that way.

"And that's when I cracked, Max. I quit caring about the case and started caring more about Margaret. And I told her the truth about why I was there, why I had gotten to know her. I told her everything."

She barreled ahead now. "I know it was wrong. I know it was stupid. And I regret it more than anything I've ever done. It was the biggest mistake of my life. It cost me my job. And worse, it cost you yours and you had nothing to do with it." She turned to face him in the shadows then, surprised and comforted that he still held her hand, even now. Their faces were close. "I know this doesn't help or change anything, but I'm so very sorry, Max. I was so wrong to let my emotions get in the way of what I was there to do, and I'm so sorry for all the harm it caused."

She waited then—for him to turn cold, or at least cool. That's how it had been on the day they'd gotten fired. And it was how he'd reacted a few days ago when she'd tried to explain. Now she finally *had* explained, and it suddenly hit her—it wasn't a very good excuse. Her emotions had gotten in the way? How utterly lame. How completely unprofessional.

"I understand," Max said softly then, slowly, as if amazed by his own words.

But he couldn't have been anymore amazed than she was. She drew back slightly, regarding him with utter astonishment. "You do?"

Beside her, he gave a short nod. "Maybe I couldn't have understood it before, even if I had let you explain it all to me. But I can understand *now* because I'm guilty of the same thing, guilty of bringing my emotions into *this* case." He lowered his voice. "Emotions for you."

Chapter Eighteen

HER STOMACH CLENCHED. Emotions for *her*? Was he talking about lust? Or…was there something else, something more?

"I owe you an apology, Kimberly," he went on. "For the times this weekend when I got angry with you. I put you in a tough position making you sexual bait for Carlo—and everything you did to reel him in worked on me instead. I haven't been very professional over the last couple of days, and I was wrong to take out my frustrations on you. But I just wanted you so damn bad and it was so hard to watch him touching you, and even harder to watch you giggling and encouraging him."

She swallowed, still unsure how he felt inside—if it was all merely sex or if anything deeper lay behind his desires. "It was my job, Max," she reminded him.

"I know," he told her. "And that's why I'm apologizing. You were doing your job and I started acting like you were doing something wrong." He paused and turned toward her, their eyes meeting in the semi-darkness. "Maybe the truth is that I expected you to do a worse job at being a seductress. I thought it would bother you more—maybe I *wanted* it to bother you more."

"It bothered me plenty, but I've gotten better at my job over the past three years."

"I've noticed." To her surprise, he gave her a small grin. "As we've discussed before, you're considerably sassier than I recall."

She shrugged. "As we've also discussed before, I found out I had to be a little tougher if I wanted to survive in this business."

"It works for you," he said. "But…"

"But what?"

"But I like the *other* you, too, Kimberly. The *softer* you."

Something in her stomach rippled. *He liked the softer her*—the her she thought of as the *real* her. And the real her was melting inside a little, wanting to succumb to his gentle words—but she thought at the moment it would be smarter to concentrate on business lest she crumble completely. "I guess this has all proven, though, that tough or not, I'm not a very good P.I."

She felt his perplexed look. "Why would you say that?"

"Because in the end, when it mattered the most, I panicked and caved in—I messed up. I was afraid of him and I let him see that." She was remembering the moment she'd uttered Max's name when he'd burst into the room and rescued her from Carlo, how it had tumbled from her lips unbidden, how desperate and afraid and needful she'd felt all at once. No matter how perfect the sight of him had been, letting Carlo see her fear had been an entirely unprofessional move.

But then Max reached up to smooth her hair with gentle fingers—and he said words she'd never thought she'd hear him say. "Some things are more important than a case, Kimberly. And I hate that I let you do that, that I let you be in that position with him."

"It's not an uncommon thing for a female P.I. to have to do, Max. You know that."

He sighed. "Of course I know that, but it's different—and a lot easier—when it's someone you don't know very well, someone you don't care for."

Max cared for her? Her body suddenly felt as if it belonged to someone else, as if—piece by piece—it was shattering in a frightening bliss that it was far too soon to feel. *But stop it. You're misunderstanding him, reading too much into his words. You must be.* Tears pressed to leak out, but she held them back. "You…care for me, Max?"

His response was to slide his arms around her, draw her close, and hold her against him like something cherished. "Kimberly," he whispered, "do you really have to ask?"

Again, she yearned to simply succumb, surrender, believe—yet she pulled back just enough to meet his eyes. Because it had been a long weekend. Full of mixed messages. "Well, yes, I *do* have to ask. I mean, after we slept together, Max, you…well, you acted…"

He silently leaned over until his forehead rested on

her shoulder. "I know," he said. "I'm sorry for that. I didn't want to admit to myself how I felt, how damn much I cared. But I *did*, Kimberly. So much that it caught me off guard."

She swallowed at the impact of his words. That sounded serious. Serious enough that she couldn't delve any deeper right now, couldn't risk finding out it wasn't really true, that it meant something less than what she was hearing. So she kept it simple and asked him the question that had haunted her all weekend. "Max?"

"Hmm?" His head still rested on her shoulder.

"Who is Julie? A...lover?"

He lifted his head and smiled into her eyes with a short, low laugh. "Julie is my neighbor. I pay her to clean my condo and do my laundry. She's sort of like a second mother to me."

"But you came out in a towel, thinking I was her."

Again, he chuckled quietly. "She's seventy years old, and believe it not, she's seen me in a towel, or less—she nursed me through a killer stomach infection with a fever of 102 last winter. She was supposed to drop my laundry off that night you came by." He gave his head a sly tilt, accompanied by a wicked little grin. "Were you jealous, babe?"

She smiled at him as she lied. "No."

And of course he could see right through her, but that was okay, because they were sharing a moment—one without need of anymore words. She still didn't know how deep his feelings for her went—after all, he'd said *wonderful* things, but he'd not exactly used the L word or anything. And, even so, it just felt good to know there was *something* mutual between them, that it wasn't one-sided, and most of all, it was incredible to know he understood now about the Carpenter case, and that he might even begin to forgive her.

HOURS PASSED AND hunger mounted. Max decided that when this was all over he was going to take Kimberly out for a lavish dinner someplace expensive. But for now, he tried not to mention food—God knew he was thinking about it, but if she wasn't, no need to make her start.

Each time he thought about leaving the closet and making a run for it, he remembered how vehement Carlo's boss had sounded when he'd insisted that they be found and it made Max stay put. Who knew how many men were out there looking for them, or waiting for them to make the mistake of showing themselves?

And just where was Frank? Enough time had passed that his old mentor should have come looking for them by now, hopefully with the police in tow. But then, who knew how often Frank checked his personal messages? Anything could have happened—the voicemail could have malfunctioned, or he might simply be out doing something fun on a Sunday afternoon and not thinking about phones or P.I. work.

"Any luck?"

The muffled voice came from just outside the closet—and Kimberly and Max both tensed, their gazes meeting.

"Nope, but the boss said to scour every nook and cranny until we find 'em. They gotta be here somewhere."

Then they heard the storage room door open.

And the vague, soft sounds of someone stepping inside, looking around.

Max squeezed Kimberly's hand, praying neither of them breathed too loud or made even the tiniest move. He hated how afraid he felt. Not afraid for himself, though Afraid for her.

His heartbeat thundered in his chest as he waited for the door to shut again, for the relief to flood him, for them to be safe once more—sort of, anyway. Seconds seemed like hours.

And that was when he suffered the horrible, unmistakable sensation of being seen. The room's stark, hollow silence did nothing to relieve the feeling, to make him think he was imagining it—instead, it only intensified his awareness.

Dread filled him as he shifted his gaze to the left and up over the wall of boxes he'd built. Carlo's eyes peered back. And he wore a leering grin. "Hi there, Max."

His chest tightened as he tensed for a fight—only then he remembered. Now Carlo had something he didn't—a gun. And the bastard chose exactly that moment to hold it up for Max to see.

"Stand up," Carlo commanded. "Both of you."

Max got to his feet and Kimberly clambered up to stand slightly behind him, as another guy appeared behind Carlo, one they hadn't seen before. "Jackpot," Carlo said with a slight glance in the new man's direction. "Clear a path, Rocko."

The man, tall and thin but sporting sizable muscles through a too-tight t-shirt, began to move some of the boxes away until no barrier stood between them.

"All right," Max said to Carlo. "You win. Just let us go and we won't tell anybody about this place."

Carlo only chuckled. "You think it's that easy?"

No, of course he didn't. But the shot had seemed worth taking. "Seems easier for *all* of us," Max pointed out. "And we've learned our lessons here—so why not let's just all go our separate ways and forget we ever met? Nice and simple."

Carlo shrugged, looking unimpressed by the suggestion. "Even if I was dumb enough to believe you, Max, not my decision to make." Then he looked around the storage area. "This seems like a safe enough spot for you until the boss gets back. No way out but the way in. And we'll be sure you don't get out *that* way, so don't even try."

"What's gonna happen when the boss gets back?" Max asked.

"Again, not my call. But if was a gambling man?" Carlo lifted the gun in his hand again, this time leveling it at Max's face, wearing a hideous smile. "Bang, bang."

Max felt all the blood drain from his cheeks, but kept

his voice steady when he asked, "What about Kimberly?"

As Carlo's gaze shifted admiringly to Max's "wife," he gave his head a regretful shake. "If it was up to me, I'd find some other way to deal with her. But the boss isn't one for taking chances."

With that, the two thugs left the room, locking them inside. And Max instinctively pulled Kimberly tight against him. Neither of them said a word. This was a high stakes operation; they knew Carlo wasn't exaggerating their fate. She slid her arms around his neck and they embraced.

"What now, Max?" she whispered, feather-soft in his ear.

He considered their options as he held her—there weren't many. "I'm not sure." He hated to admit that, but it was the truth.

And when she pulled back just far enough for him to see her pretty face, he lifted one hand to her cheek. "I'm so sorry, Kimberly."

She peered up into his eyes and shook her head. "No, Max, don't be sorry. Because it's not your fault. And because I'm not giving up yet. I refuse to believe this is over."

Even amid their despair, he managed a small smile for her. "This is that tough, sassy side of you I like."

And their gazes held and he saw in Kimberly's...a fresh heat—a heat he recognized, a heat now tempered with a primitive sort of fear. They might very well die soon. This wasn't a comic book, not pretend—this was as real as it got.

His heartbeat increased as he let himself be absorbed into those pretty eyes of hers. In the shadowy light of the closet, they were so dark as to be almost colorless, yet they still shone hot upon him, and he could see in her all he ever had—all the beauty, all the grace, all the sweetness, and all the raw sexuality, now magnified with the need that accompanied it.

Max couldn't wait another second—he crushed a hard kiss to her silken lips, and she returned it, wild and needful, her arms twining around his neck as she leaned fully into him, her warmth intoxicating.

And then they were sinking to the floor together, and she was climbing into his lap, straddling him until his erection pressed up into that most tender part of her. "I need you, babe," he murmured.

A small, reckless moan left her, but he stifled it with another kiss, his tongue pressing hungrily past her lips. And one hot kiss turned into another, and another—until finally their kisses became less frantic, calming into a slower sort of passion, deep and consuming, yet still just as desperate.

"I need you, too, Max." Her words came in the gentlest of whispers, a verbal caress. "I need you so much."

They touched tongues delicately and he slid one hand to her perfect breast. Finding her nipple through her dress and bra, he gently pinched, squeezed, between thumb and forefinger. Another tiny moan escaped her, but he cut this one off with his mouth, as well, still teasing the taut peak with rhythmic strokes of his thumb.

They were both panting now, quiet and harsh, and he feared he would burst with the intensity of of how much he wanted her. Of how badly his body *needed* her. That was how it had always been with Kimberly—it took so little to set him on fire for her, and once there was fire, the flames were hard to extinguish. But this wasn't just about his body. No, this was way more than physical.

"Remember before," he said, short of breath, "when we stopped? Because of where we were?"

She nodded, their gazes seductively close, her eyes wide with want.

"Well, where we are doesn't matter anymore, Kimberly," he told her. "Or maybe it's just the opposite and it matters more than anything. But either way, nothing could stop me from having you now."

Chapter Nineteen

MAX HAD NEVER wanted anything in his life as badly as he wanted Kimberly, right now. The feel of her, the scent of her, was enough to bury him.

She answered his words with a feverish kiss, long and feverish and filled with all the heat the two of them always managed to generate together.

But he wanted even more than that from her. "Tell me," he growled in her ear.

"Tell you what?" she whispered.

"Tell me you want me inside you."

An erotic sigh escaped her, and her voice came weak and breathy. "Yes, I want you inside me. I want you deep, deep inside me."

And then she gazed intensely into his eyes, her own voracious with desire—but also commanding him, with a silent fervor: *Don't play any more games, don't ask me to say anything else. Just do it.*

Planting his hands on her hips, he pulled her down to meet him, drinking in more of that sexy aggressiveness as she began to grind against him in a hard, sensual rhythm. He worked at the buttons on her dress as she moved, then pushed the fabric aside. Parting the lace of her bra, he reached in to caress her full, round breasts. Damn, he had missed them. Missed *this*. Missed all of her.

When a low moan slipped past her lush lips, though, he kissed her to quiet it. They *had* to keep quiet. And the next thing he knew, she was biting his lower lip—just a little, just enough to shoot a heightened bolt of longing through him, making him even harder for her than he already was. And then *he* wanted to moan and it killed him to hold it in. So he clenched his teeth and closed his eyes and leaned his forehead against hers, all while she gyrated against him in hot little circles.

"I need you in me *now*."

The words came as gentle as a leaf wafting from a tree, but the urgency in them nearly paralyzed him. He needed to be in her, too—as soon as possible.

Grazing his hands up her thighs and under her dress, he soon found more lace beneath his fingertips. Smoothly, he slid his fingers inside the thin strip of it at her hip, taking firm hold—and then he gave one brisk yank, ripping the lace free. Her gasp filled him with a perverse and powerful pleasure before he rasped, "Unzip me."

Her ragged breath alone was enough to drive him wild as she lifted off him and undid his shorts. "Hurry," he prodded her, his own voice sounding so throaty he barely recognized it. And when—sweet Jesus—she reached inside and took hold of him, he let out a rough gasp of his own.

But then, to his surprise, she went still, pinning him in place again with her intent gaze. He waited, impatient as a teenager, practically pulsing in her fist—but tried to calm himself by reaching up to brush a strand of hair from her face.

When she finally spoke, her voice came out sounding broken. "Max, there's...no one else I'd rather..."

He couldn't bear to watch her struggle with the words, so he stopped her with a truth of his own. "I know, love. Me, too."

And then there was no more waiting—she was lowering herself onto him, taking him deep, deep inside her. And she was releasing another of those long, low moans as he filled her, and lovely though the sound was, right now he had no choice but to reach up and cover her mouth with his hand.

Only then his fingers ended up in her mouth and she was sucking them as she began to move on him again, now with him in her, and he starting losing track of space, time, reality. All he knew was that Kimberly had taken control and was making love to him. Sweet, slow, desperate love. Using her whole body, her whole self, her undulations driven by a smoldering hunger he'd never witnessed in her before. And he was basking in it, letting it happen, watching her love him, pushing up into her, wanting her to feel it all the way to her very core.

Biting her lip, she arched toward him, her lovely coral-tipped breasts near his face, and he took one pebbled nipple in his mouth as she continued in those slow, sexy circles—and then he felt her coming, her body convulsing over him, around him, her sweet tiny sounds too faint to need to muffle this time, and too beautiful to want to.

As she collapsed against him, he wrapped his arms around her, awed by everything passionate and beautiful about her—when he came, too, in shocking waves of heat that made him shudder against her limp body in his arms. "Oh God, babe," he whispered, breathless.

"I love you, Max," she said, her breath hot on his ear.

And his chest clenched slightly.

He tightened his hold on her. But he didn't say it back.

Because he wasn't quite ready to hear those words. Even as he let his heart fill with them.

He just prayed she understood, prayed she knew how much he felt in this moment, prayed it would be enough to get her—get them *both*—through the night.

And at the same time, he prayed desperately that there would be a tomorrow.

AT SOME POINT, they both slept. Slept until he awakened her with kisses—kisses to her shoulder, to the curve of her breast. And then she climbed onto him again in the confines of their hiding place, and she stayed faultlessly quiet, but he could almost feel the exquisite torture of her silence as she moved against him.

Hours later, he awoke once more, blissfully satisfied. And before even opening his eyes, he found himself ruminating about yesterday morning after their sex. He saw her dreamy eyes and romantic expression next to him in bed. He hadn't been ready for it then—but he was a lot more prepared for it now. After what they'd been through together in the last twenty-four hours, he felt closer to her than ever.

And he'd finally forgiven her for the Carpenter case on top of it all.

He didn't know how or when exactly, but somehow through the course of the day yesterday, he'd let go of his hurtful grudge. Just let it drift away. He'd realized it didn't matter anymore, that she'd done the best she could at the time, just like we all do in life.

He wished he'd told her now, before they'd had sex last night. Even if he hadn't been able to say *I love you*, *I forgive you* might have been almost as good under the strange circumstances of their relationship. And he knew he could probably be better at expressing emotions and all that, but...well, maybe he'd work on that after they got out of *this*. Right now he had other things to concentrate on.

Like figuring out what they were going to do.

And before that, waking her and drinking in that dreamy look in her morning eyes.

Although it wasn't quite morning *yet*—his backlit watch read 4:30 a.m. Still, he didn't want them sleeping any later—if they were to formulate any kind of plan, they'd better get started. He nudged her softly, waiting as she slowly lifted her head from his shoulder and eased her eyes open.

Then she turned to face him, their gazes connecting in the shadowy air. "Geez, Tate, did you have to rip off my panties?"

He flinched, stunned. Okay, that wasn't exactly dreamy, or romantic. Maybe he didn't know her as well as he thought—she was becoming less predictable by the day. "Well, you didn't seem to mind at the time," he pointed out.

"I was feeling…a bit desperate."

He raised his eyebrows in her direction. "Has your situation changed in some way I don't know about?"

Kimberly's situation hadn't changed, but her attitude definitely had. After last night with Max, it would have been easy to wake up feeling all lovey-dovey. But she knew a lot about herself, and one thing she knew for sure was that lovey-dovey would make her weak and spineless and girlish—and if they were to stay alive, she needed her professional wits about her today.

So she'd decided to put on her game face bright and early, without giving her spongier side time to start absorbing everything she felt when she looked into his eyes. Max had said yesterday that he liked the tough side of her. Well, today that was what he'd get. It was imperative if they were to have any hope of getting out of this mess with their lives.

"We need a plan, Tate."

"I'm fresh out at the moment, Brandt."

"Well, I'm not. Listen up." Her change in attitude had injected her with a fresh shot of strength that had her feeling bolder than she could have imagined under the circumstances.

"I'm listening," he said.

"There's a heat duct overhead." She pointed at it.

"True enough."

"And so I'm thinking—what if we could somehow crawl through it and get out? They do it in the movies all the time."

"I don't know, Brandt—this isn't a movie. And that thing looks like it was manufactured in the Dark Ages. I think in the movies they use sturdier-looking heat ducts."

"Maybe so. But do you have any better ideas? Besides, it's the middle of the night. They might have let their guard down, expecting us to be asleep. If we're gonna do something, it seems like now's the time."

He tilted his head as he gazed at her in the half-light. "That's your plan?"

"Look, we can stay here and wait for Carlo's boss to shoot us, or we can take a chance in the heat duct. I say we go now and be done with it, one way or the other."

Max didn't like it—he was generally big on *orchestrating* a plan, giving it some thought first. After all, a little spontaneity on his part is what had landed them in this predicament.

Still, she made sense. There was nothing to be gained by waiting. And the cover of darkness sure couldn't hurt.

The rusty heat duct looked like it was ready to disintegrate on top of them, but it might be their only hope.

"All right, Brandt—you've convinced me."

"One more thing," she said. "Another part of my plan."

"Let's hear it."

"If we end up out of the heat duct and on the floor, and we bump into just one guy, split up."

He blinked, scowled. "Where the hell's the logic in that?"

"One person can't shoot both of us at the same time."

He let out an incredulous breath. He *really* didn't like this. If they were going to get shot at, he had every intention of making sure he was the one who took the bullet.

"And," she added, "the guy will probably be keeping his gun stuffed in his pants behind his back, right? So if one of us could possibly get behind him—"

Okay, he was crazy about the woman, but... "Brandt, that's too far-fetched. Like I said before, this isn't a movie."

"It's not far-fetched at all," she corrected him. "I saw Carlo pull his gun from there when we were out in the warehouse."

Max sighed, taking that in but still not quite willing to concede. "Okay, so you've impressed me with your observational skills. Still, if we get caught, we stick together. No arguments."

She sneered at him, but he didn't care.

"Got it?" he asked.

Kimberly let out a heavy breath and then, hesitantly, nodded. But she made sure to let him see the irritation in her eyes.

As they both got to their feet, she sensed them both silently steeling themselves for what was to come. Max glanced over at her. "Ready to do this?"

She nodded again. "Although, frankly, Tate, I'd feel better if I had underwear on."

This time *he* sneered at *her*. And they exchanged looks of annoyance—just like old times. Well, old times over the past few days. But it had been a hell of a long weekend.

She watched as he carefully climbed up on a tower of boxes toward a metal slat in the duct that was partially disconnected from the rest, the screws missing. After a few minutes of working at it, it finally came off completely, opening an entryway to the duct.

"I'll go first," he announced, and she knew he was thinking about protecting her—if it was going to come crashing down beneath the added weight, he wanted to be the one to fall, not her.

And while her P.I.'s sensibilities were slightly offended, her feminine ones were not, so she simply said, "Okay," and waited as he pulled himself easily up into the duct with the agility of a cat. When he disappeared inside and the duct didn't move or even sag, she hoped that meant it was stronger than it looked.

Next, she followed his path up the boxes and into the duct. It wasn't easy in a dress, but soon she was in the pitch black tunnel on her hands and knees.

Reaching out to make sure he was in front of her, she found his butt.

"Geez, Brandt. Not now."

"Quit dreaming," she snipped. "It was an accident."

"Are you in? Are we ready to crawl?"

"More than ready. Let's get going."

The travel was slow, cramped, and uncomfortable. Breathing was difficult—while she could see nothing, she could smell, taste, and feel the heavy dust particles all around her. Moving through the unrelenting blackness was nearly unbearable, but she tried not to feel claustrophobic or think about the possibility that bugs or vermin could be sharing the space with them.

After a few long minutes, she had no idea how far they had gone, and she only prayed they were making progress in some direction that would bring this to a happy conclusion soon.

Soon took longer than she wanted, though. *Get me out of here. Get me out of here. Get me out of here.* Her chest grew almost unbearably tight as a sense of panic began to set in.

But be calm. Be tough. That tougher you who gets the job done. You have no other choice right now. If ever in your life you need to be strong, this is it.

"You all right?" Max asked after a little while.

"Yes," she lied.

"I don't believe you."

She tried to take a deep breath but couldn't. "I'm tough, remember? Now shut up and keep going."

"I'm here with you, babe," he said.

And she knew he *got* it, *all* of it, that he understood she was miserable and afraid right now, and that no matter how intent she was on not letting it show, on staying strong, he wanted to help her get through this. "I know," she answered softly. "And…I'm glad."

"Soon this will all be over, and we'll be safe and sound." His tone remained reassuring.

"Do you really think that?"

He hesitated a beat too long. "Yes."

"Now *I* don't believe *you*."

"Yes you do. You have to, Brandt. You haven't given up, or you wouldn't have suggested the heat duct. So just keep going, and just think about how good it will feel to see the sun again and get back to normal life."

Normal life. *Normal life without you? Or…an old, better kind of normal?* They'd only been a couple for less than six months, but it had felt so right, had so quickly become just that, normal. Life had never *really* felt normal since.

As they kept crawling, it gave her some sense of hope to realize he'd actually succeeded in distracting her from the fact that they were in a hot, narrow, smothering heat duct—or at least he had for a little while. *But just keep staying calm. Just for a little longer* Remembering that this was a life or death situation helped.

"Damn," Max whispered in front of her then.

She didn't have to ask why. She'd already caught sight of the rectangle of dim light ahead.

"The duct is ending," he told her anyway. And when he approached the opening a minute later and peered down, he quietly announced, "We're right in the middle of the damn warehouse."

But Kimberly simply took a deep breath. Kept being tough. Believing. "At least we're out of the storage room," she reminded him.

"Good point," he sent back over his shoulder. "We're gonna have to get down to the floor now somehow, Brandt. And then we're gonna have to find our way out, quick and quiet. Ready?"

"Do you have a plan for this?"

"Not really."

"Then what are you doing?" The duct was wider here, and he appeared to be squeezing his legs around to the front, toward the opening.

"Winging it," he said. After which he made a quick, simple drop down to the floor—and again, she thought the movement looked like that of a cat. Astonishingly, he'd made the ten-foot jump gracefully and had landed with barely a noise.

"Max," she whispered down to him. "I can't do that like you just did. I'll break my legs."

But below her, he was shaking his head and looking annoyed. "This is no time to go soft on me, Brandt. Just do it. Don't think about it. I'll break your fall."

He was right. So she didn't think. She just took a deep breath and let herself drop.

He kept his word and let her fall onto him, the impact knocking him down. But despite the rough landing, she ended up in his arms, and they both scrambled to their feet, uninjured other than a few scratches and bruises picked up along the way.

Now on the floor, she looked around. Everything was gloriously still. And not as dark as she might have hoped, but it remained much more shadowy than it would be in the morning when sunlight came blasting through the windows near the ceiling. They'd picked a good time to go.

Her stomach churned with nervousness as they began silently making their way around heaps of glassware containers. The place was big and maze-like, making it hard to get their bearings or have much of a sense where they were going. But they kept moving, quiet and swift—and a few tenuous moments later, they rounded a row of crates and, to her amazement, she spotted the door, the very same one they'd come through yesterday afternoon.

Her heart pounded even harder than it already was as she grabbed Max's wrist and pointed. As his eyes lit with relief, she knew she wasn't just imagining it; it wasn't just some strange warehouse mirage—it was the right door, their means of escape. And the normalcy he'd promised her waited just on the other side. *We're actually getting out of here!*

"Well, what do we have here?"

Oh shit. Kimberly and Max both turned to find Carlo standing behind them.

"I don't know how you two got out of that room, but you might as well have stayed put, because you sure as hell aren't getting out of this building."

A ragged, disbelieving sigh slipped past her lips. And part of her wanted to break down and cry in despair. She was so damn tired—physically and emotionally. She wasn't sure she had any more strength left inside her.

But another part of her quickly realized that Carlo was alone.

And what had she told Max? If they went up against only one person, they should separate.

He'd practically forbidden it, but she didn't care. She had to trust her instincts now—she could see no other way.

So she strode boldly toward Carlo without giving Max even a glance—she only prayed he'd stay where he was.

"Brandt," he snapped, low, but at least he didn't seem to be following her.

Meanwhile, Carlo took a step back, obviously confused by her approach. "What the hell…?" he muttered. And she began to wonder if maybe he would make this easy—maybe she could just walk up and take his gun herself.

But then he reached for it—pulling it from the back of his waistband, just as she'd known he would.

Instead of letting that stop her, though, she remained unfazed and kept walking toward him—which clearly confounded him all the more. "Hold still!" he said.

"You wouldn't really hurt me, Carlo," she said with a purr in her voice, "would you?" She was relying on what she knew to be his weakness: women, sex, seduction.

He seemed unable to decide whether to hold the gun on her or Max, although he ultimately chose Max—figuring him to be more adversarial, she guessed—yet his eyes had gone soft at her provocative tone.

"Would you?" she whispered again. And then she was at his side, so close she could have reached up and kissed him, and she knew he was thinking the same thing.

"I...don't want to hurt you, Kimberly," he said, sounding nervous. "You know that."

"Yes, I do know that," she breathed, letting her eyes widen, meeting his gaze, and trying to figure out exactly how she could get that gun from his hand.

But then Max said, "Damn it, Brandt, get away from him."

And Carlo swung his gaze back to Max. "Get your hands where I can see 'em!" After which she heard him mutter under his breath. "And who the hell's Brandt?"

Before Carlo could figure out what to do next, her eyes landed on one of the heavy white pitchers they'd found yesterday, jutting from the packing straw in an open bin—and she picked it up, lifted it high with both hands, and brought it crashing down on Carlo's head.

The smarmy crook crumpled to the ground before

her, and she was on the verge of feeling victorious—when she caught sight of the alarm shining in Max's eyes. Damn it, what now?

That was when someone behind her said, "Hold it right there!"

The words halted her in place, but she cautiously looked over her shoulder to find three men with guns, all of them pointed at her and Max. Her heart dropped to her stomach.

Still, she knew instantly that they'd come too far to give in now, and that their only chance lay in blatant and very risky defiance. The only other alternative was certain death. So she looked toward Max, her back still to the gunmen. And she moved her lips to say *Run*.

Yet Max just stood there, his eyes darting back and forth between her and the gunmen. And she supposed he was determined to do something to save her, to treat her as the damsel in distress she'd once been. *But Max, there's no time for that now.* She had to force the issue. She mouthed the word to him again, this time with fire in her eyes. *Run!*

Then she bolted madly toward the door and Max joined her. Gunfire erupted behind them, with bullets whizzing past and people yelling and danger so thick she could taste it.

A sharp pain exploded in her hip and she looked down to see a bright red blot on her dress. She kept running in spite of it, although she felt strange and weak and heavy. And as they neared the door, she yelled at Max, "Tate, I've been shot!"

Chapter Twenty

SHE'D BEEN SHOT? His Kimberly? No, it couldn't be. But a glance told Max it was true. Blood stained the side of her dress. And everything turned to slow motion for him.

"Can you keep going?" he yelled to her.

"I think so."

They were at the door, Max pushing her through, running behind her. *I've got to get her safe, I've got to get her safe*. Nothing else mattered.

And then he looked up and saw the pre-dawn street before him illuminated with eerie swirling lights—blue ones, on cop cars. They lined the front of the warehouse.

"Max! Kim!" The voice belonged to Frank, rising from somewhere amid the blue glow.

And then there was more gunfire behind them and Max tackled Kimberly, pushing her to the pavement, praying that it would all end soon, and that she wouldn't die—*please don't let her die, God. Please*.

"THANKS AGAIN, FRANK," Max said, clasping his friend's hand outside the warehouse. "If you hadn't gotten that message and called the police in, I'm just not sure…"

"Hey, let's not think about that, huh?" Frank slapped him on the back and it helped him lighten up a little. Still, Frank had really come through for them—a little late, but better than never. He and Kimberly were out of danger, and Carlo and all his buddies were on their way to jail.

And Kimberly had come through, too. She'd defied him by doing just the opposite of what he'd told her to when they'd confronted Carlo, but it had turned out to be a pretty good move. Still risky as hell, but if those *other* guys hadn't come along, they'd have been home free.

As he parted with Frank and made his way through the chaos still churning all around him at the crime scene, he couldn't stop thinking about her bravery.

A moment later, he kneeled next to her in an ambulance that was about to take her away to the hospital. She'd sustained only a flesh wound, thank God, but she was wearing it like her very own red badge of courage as she lay stretched out on a gurney. "Can you believe I actually got shot, Max?" she asked with a huge smile as an EMT cleaned and bandaged the scratches she'd gotten when Max tackled her.

He wanted to laugh and he wanted to cry. He'd never seen anyone so happy about a gunshot wound. But he should have learned this weekend that if anyone could catch him off guard, it was her. He brushed back a lock of hair from her face.

"I wonder if I'll have a scar. I normally hate scars, but in this case, it might be kind of cool." She shifted her gaze to the young man currently pressing an adhesive bandage across her forehead. "Will I have one?"

"Probably," he said, his smile tinged with amusement.

Her expression said she was pleased with his answer.

When the EMT was done, Max said, "Can we have a minute?"

The young man gave a friendly nod, then stepped out and closed the ambulance doors.

And upon being alone with her for the first time since their escape, all Max's emotions came rushing back. He wanted to kill her. And he wanted to kiss her.

He chose the second, leaning over to cup her silken cheek in one palm before delivering a slow, deep kiss that he hoped she felt as much as he did.

"I'm sorry about knocking you down," he told her after the kiss was through. "You didn't need that on top of being shot."

"It's all right—I know you were only trying to protect me. And besides, compared to taking a bullet, they're pretty minimal injuries." She was smiling again.

"Does it hurt?" he asked of the wound.

"A little. But I feel…validated, you know?" Her eyes sparkled. "Like a real P.I."

Though with a tilt of his head, he assured her, "You

were already a real P.I., Kimberly."

She gazed up at him, quiet and thoughtful-looking. "Really, Max? Do you truly feel that way?"

He nodded. "Completely, babe. And you're damn good at your job."

Another small smile graced her face. "Thank you."

"Well, I'd better let them get you to the hospital."

"Yeah," she agreed quietly.

"I'll…see you soon."

As Max exited the ambulance, then watched it pull away up the neglected street, he thought there was probably more he should have said. But he had no idea what it was.

KIMBERLY LAY IN the hospital bed that afternoon, wanting to admire the bandages on her wound, but they were hidden beneath the white gown she wore.

"Hey."

She looked up to find Max standing in her doorway bearing a vase of bright summer flowers and looking as handsome as ever. She was both happy and sad to see him—happy because after a few hours apart, the very sight of him turned her to jelly, and sad because she knew a lot of hurt lay ahead. Things would change now; they'd go their separate ways. If she'd had any hopes otherwise, they'd pretty much died after their rescue by the police. She'd immediately been able to tell that "back to normal" meant going on with their lives as they had before this weekend.

But, well…if lust and some partnerly affection was all there would ever be between them, at least she and Max had made peace. Amazingly hot, sensual, mind-blowing peace. She would always long for more, but she couldn't make him feel something he didn't.

"Hi," she said. "Pretty flowers."

"For a pretty lady," he said, setting them on the table next to the bed.

"Even now?" she asked, thinking of the scratches and scrapes on her forehead and chin.

"Even now," he told her. "I'd go so far as to say always."

The words touched her—but for some reason, she played them off as teasing. "Always, huh? That's a pretty big step to take, Tate. Sure you're ready to go that far?"

"For you, baby," he teased her back, "I'd go anywhere."

Those words tugged at her heart, too, and she wished it wasn't all just playful banter.

"So tell me," she said, changing the subject, "what was the deal with Carlo? Who did he work for?"

"Turns out Dormer and Sons is a legitimate shipping business like you thought, or at least *partially* legitimate. Apparently, old man Dormer—the boss guy we had the displeasure of meeting—has had mob connections since he was young, but he didn't tie that part of his life in with his business until a few years ago when he quit turning much of a profit. His mob friends suggested that a shipping business would be a convenient way to smuggle stolen jewelry. Apparently, the jewels went to to different cities all over the world, where they were sold on the black market. The bulk of glassware that leaves the warehouse, though, is just that—glassware."

"Wow," she said. "So we nabbed a major crook."

Max smiled and gave her a short nod.

"And what about Carlo in specific?" Kimberly asked. "Where does *he* fit in?"

"He's one of about a dozen low-level guys Dormer hired to do his dirty work. Got into the business when his father—a wealthy playboy type, also with a few mob connections—died without leaving him a penny. Carlo's mistake, though, was his fascination with tying seduction in with thievery—it made his crimes stand out from the rest. Which was where we entered the picture.

"But enough about cops and robbers for today," Max concluded. "How are you feeling?"

"Good," she assured him. "A little tired, but not bad under the circumstances."

"I could use some rest myself," he replied. "But I wanted to stop by and check on you first."

She kept smiling. "That's sweet of you."

And it was. But sweet was not love. Sweet was…respect, and care, and that newfound peace between them. And she knew the longer he was there, the sadder she would be when he finally left. She might truly be tough inside, but where Max was concerned, she was as helpless as ever. Funny that their rescue—

Godsend that it had been—had also been the end of things between them. "Well, I'm fine," she said. "And it was nice of you to bring the flowers—I'll enjoy them. But I know we're both tired, so you're...free to go."

Next to her, Max hesitated. And as she peered into those dark, beautiful eyes of his, she could have sworn she saw a tiny hint of indecision—but not much. Not enough to count.

"One more thing, Brandt," he said.

"What's that?"

"I want to tell you that I meant it earlier when I said you really are a good P.I. And I want to tell you, too, that I...forgive you. For the Carpenter case. For the whole job thing."

Wow. Trying to wrap her head around that—because she knew, for Max, to say something like that was huge—she took a deep breath and imparted the same teasing words as before, but this time she meant them. "That's a pretty big step to take, Tate. Sure you're ready to go that far?"

He nodded, no hesitation this time. "Yeah. I am."

"Thank you, Max. That means a lot to me."

And it truly *did*.

But she wanted so much more than that from him now, and with each passing second, that yearning grew. And the sad truth was—it just wasn't going to happen.

"You should go get some sleep," she managed.

Max gave a slight nod, then squeezed her hand in parting before walking out the door.

And as a solitary tear rolled down her cheek while she gazed at the empty doorway, she realized that she'd finally learned to read Max's eyes. And they'd just told her goodbye.

MAX WALKED DOWN the crisp white hospital corridor, preparing to get in his car, go home, and climb into bed for a week. It sounded so easy, so restful. And so...*oddly empty*.

Where the hell had *that* thought come from?

And when he really examined it, things started looking emptier with each step he took. After all, what was waiting for him at home? An empty condo. What waited at work? A job that, at the moment, seemed almost as empty. It *all* suddenly seemed empty...*without her*.

Are you crazy? Keep walking, dude.

So that was what he did, pushing his way through a revolving door and out into the southern California heat. He headed toward the parking lot where he'd left his Porsche—even if a part of him wanted to go back.

But just keep walking. Because that's what you do, it's how you play your life. And he had a *good* life, all things considered. He had the life he wanted.

And so he still kept moving, putting one foot in front of the other.

But she stayed on his mind. Everything about this weekend was on his mind. Every good moment—with her. Hell, she was enough to make him forget they'd actually almost been killed.

What are you running from?

After all, hadn't he forgiven her? Yes. But this was about more than that. This...was about sharing his life with somebody. Really sharing it. He'd tried that before, and it had gone bad in a big way. Forgiving and forgetting were two different things.

But if you keep walking, you'll never see her again. Never brush another strand of hair away from that pretty face. Never hear that sweet laughter. Never gaze on the seductive heat in her eyes.

"I'm being too damn dramatic here," he muttered to himself as he opened his car door. If he wanted to see her again, later, he could. He knew where she lived, after all. So he could take his time, think about this, decide if it was a good idea.

But the truth was, he knew that if he got in the car and drove away from this hospital, it would create a certain distance, physically and emotionally. A guy didn't have to go all the way to Vegas to leave somebody behind. If he left now, it would be for good.

A lot of moments over the last day had seemed like pivotal ones. Pivotal in bringing down the bad guys. Then, later, pivotal in saving his and Kimberly's lives. But he had the oddest feeling that he'd just landed right in the middle of another critical moment, where what he did would count for a long time to come.

Get in the car, dude. Drive away. No crime in that.

And there are a lot of women in the world. You want a

woman—you can find one who hasn't already brought down your whole damn life. So why take the risk?

He got in the car, shut the door, started the engine. Thought again of his bed and how good it was going to feel there. *Just go home and sleep this off. It'll all look clearer, better, in the morning. A little distance was a good thing. A little planning was, too.*

Only one problem with any of that. None of the other women in the world were Kimberly Brandt.

"I CAN'T LEAVE." He approached her hospital bed to see...damn, was she crying?

"Why not?" she said through a sniffle. "Car won't start?"

His heart drummed against his chest. "No—it's you, Kimberly."

"What *about* me?" She dabbed at her eyes with a tissue.

"I love to argue with you," he said.

"What?"

"It's insane, I know, but I love it."

She simply stared at him, obviously waiting for him to say something that made sense. He wasn't doing very well so far. So much for being impetuous again, but he had to forge on because he only had one shot at making this right. "And I love to have hot, sweaty sexy with you," he said.

She still looked baffled. And he knew he was still doing a lousy job, but he'd never actually done this before—he was new at it. "So you're saying…what?" she asked.

Just tell her. Just spit it out.

"I'm saying that I love you." Wow. He stopped, shook his head, amazed at how easy that had been. "God, that felt good. To just say it. I'm pretty sure I've loved you for…well, a long time. It just took this weekend to make me see it, accept it. I've missed you, babe, and I don't want to let you get away again."

She blinked. "You don't?"

"No, I don't." Then he took a deep breath and blurted out the next part. "Marry me."

"Huh?"

Okay, now she was making this difficult. "You heard me, Brandt. I want to marry you. I want to feel like I feel when I'm around you all the time, for the rest of my life."

"You do?" She was blinking some more now, and trembling a little, and he suddenly thought that maybe, just maybe, this wasn't such a new idea to her.

"I really do," he said. "Will you? Marry me, Kimberly?"

"Oh, Max—yes! Yes, yes, yes!"

And then he was on the bed with her without really planning it, taking her into his arms, kissing her soft and warm and deep, and whispering, "This feels a hell of a lot better than being at home in bed alone," and then, "Aw hell, am I hurting you?" when he remembered her wound.

But she only shook her head, laughing—that pretty laughter he'd been afraid he'd never hear again, that pretty laughter that had drawn him back here to this perfect moment.

Kimberly almost didn't believe it. It was too wonderful to be true. She gazed up into Max's handsome face, into those dark, sexy eyes she'd just learned to read, and what she saw there was…love. Just like the door back at the warehouse, this was real, no mirage. "Oh, Max," she breathed, "I've loved you for so long. And I never thought you'd love me back."

"How could I not? You're…everything, Kimberly. Soft and sweet. Smart and tough. Hot and sexy—and amazing in bed on top of it all. What man could resist all that?"

She sighed with joy, glad the tough part of her was for real, glad the soft part of her was still intact, and glad he loved all of her. Then she twined her arms around his neck and pulled him into another long, languid kiss as he smoothly ran his hands up under her hospital gown.

"You don't have any panties on, Brandt."

She bit her lip coquettishly. "My partner ripped them off when we were having hot sex last night."

He raised his eyebrows at the reminder. "Any chance you're up for a repeat performance?"

Kimberly laughed. "I thought you were tired."

But Max was already off the bed and closing the door, then sliding the visitor's chair in front of it. Returning to the bed, he flashed a devilish grin. "Not *that* tired, babe."

Epilogue

"I NEED A woman."

"You've got a beautiful one right there."

Frank pointed across his living room toward Kimberly in her bridal gown. He'd given her away at the ceremony and was now hosting the wedding reception.

Max smiled and took a moment to study her himself. After all, they'd only have one wedding day and she looked beautiful.

That was why he hated to muddy the day with business. But he'd just gotten an urgent call this morning from a client who needed some undercover work done. The job could wait until they returned from their honeymoon to Hawaii in two weeks, but he'd have to start making some arrangements now, before they left.

"It's for a job," Max explained.

"What are the parameters?"

"The usual," he replied. "Smart, good instincts, good acting abilities. And she needs to be attractive, too."

"Like I said, Max, you've got a beautiful woman right there."

He located Kimberly across the floor again—she was dancing to a Leon Redbone song with his father. The sight brought a smile to his face, but he let it fade as he turned back to Frank. "It's a dangerous job."

"She's a capable woman."

"The job calls for a guy, too," Max said.

"And you're a capable guy."

"But I'm getting out of the field, remember?"

"What's going on over here?" Apparently, the dance with his dad had ended because Kimberly had just bounded up the steps to the foyer where the two men stood. She planted her hands on her hips. "You look way too worried for your wedding day, Max."

"It's like this," Frank said before Max could even begin to reply. "He's got a dangerous job lined up that he's afraid to let you take. Oh, and there'll be a male partner involved, too, and he's too jealous to let you work with anyone but him, but he refuses to do it himself because he wants to quit."

"How many times do I have to tell you, Frank? I'm not quitting—I'm taking a step back."

"Quitting," Frank said.

"How dare you!" Kimberly jumped in. "Whatever that job is, I want it! And I want you to do it with me! Got it?"

Max tossed a glance at Frank. "There's that sassy side I told you about."

"I like it," Frank said.

"So," she said, "are we square on this? We're doing

this together?"

Max tilted his head. "You remember what happened the last time we worked together, babe. I didn't handle it well. I let my emotions—"

"Get in the way," she finished for him. "Yes, I know." Then she reached up and kissed him on the cheek. "But you're a good P.I., Tate. You'll learn."

He couldn't help smiling.

"So do we have a deal? As soon as the honeymoon's over, we go to work together?"

Max sighed, then gazed into her eyes, today a stunning shade of emerald that sparkled when she smiled. "Oh, what the hell," he said. "Who wants to quit anyway?"

Look for more classic Toni Blake reissues, including:

The Cinderella Scheme
The Guy Next Door
The Bewitching Hour

And don't miss any of these contemporary romance titles from Toni Blake:

The Coral Cove Series:
All I Want Is You
Love Me If You Dare
Take Me All The Way

The Destiny Series:
One Reckless Summer
Sugar Creek
Whisper Falls
Holly Lane
Willow Springs
Half Moon Hill
Christmas in Destiny

Other Titles:
Wildest Dreams
The Red Diary
Letters to a Secret Lover
Tempt Me Tonight
Swept Away

About the Author

Toni Blake's love of writing began when she won an essay contest in the fifth grade. Soon after, she penned her first novel, nineteen notebook pages long. Since then, Toni has become a RITA™-nominated author of more than twenty contemporary romance novels, her books have received the National Readers Choice Award and Bookseller's Best Award, and her work has been excerpted in *Cosmo*. Toni lives in the Midwest and enjoys traveling, crafts, and spending time outdoors.

Learn more about Toni and her books at www.toniblake.com, or sign up for her newsletter and follow her on Facebook to get all the latest news and have a chance to win signed books and other prizes.

Made in the USA
Lexington, KY
15 June 2017